THE SWAP

George Layton is an actor and a writer. He has appeared in many productions in New York, Australia and in the West End, his favourite role being Fagin in *Oliver!* at the London Palladium. He has also starred in many television programmes, including *Minder, Doctor in the House, It Ain't Half Hot, Mum,* and *Robin's Nest,* many of which he wrote. He has created and written numerous successful TV comedies which are shown all over the world, including *Don't Wait Up, Executive Stress* and *Friday Night Fever.*

The Swap is George Layton's second book. His first, *The Fib,* has sold over a quarter of a million copies. He lives in London with his family and two dogs, who rely on him totally – the dogs that is.

Books by George Layton

The Fib and Other Stories
The Swap and Other Stories

THE SWAP
and Other Stories

George Layton

MACMILLAN CHILDREN'S BOOKS

First published 1997 by Macmillan Children's Books

This edition published 1998 by Macmillan Children's Books
a division of Macmillan Publishers Limited
25 Eccleston Place, London SW1W 9NF
and Basingstoke

Associated companies throughout the world

ISBN 0 330 35028 5

3 5 7 9 8 6 4

A CIP catalogue record for this book is available from
the British Library.

Phototypeset by Intype London Ltd
Printed and bound in Great Britain by Mackays of Chatham plc, Kent

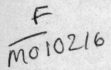

In memory of my dear parents
Edith and Freddie Layton
and
to the City of Bradford
that made them so welcome

CONTENTS

THE TREEHOUSE

The first time I ever saw Mr Bleasdale take the register, I couldn't take my eyes off him. That was because he didn't take his eye off me. Yes – his eye. His left eye.

It was on my first day at Grammar School and I'd never seen anything like it. I'd been put in 1B and Mr Bleasdale was our form master. He also taught Latin and he could look down with one eye to read, write or take the register and at the same time could keep his other eye on the class. And it never blinked. It just stared at us making sure nobody misbehaved while he was calling out our names.

'Barraclough . . .'

'Yes, sir!'

'Boocock . . .'

'Yes, sir.'

'Cawthra . . .'

'Sir . . .'

Everybody answered when they heard their name called out. Nobody dared to look round to see what the lad shouting out looked like.

We were all nervous anyway, it being our first day at the Grammar, but none of us had seen anything like this. We just sat staring straight ahead at Mr Bleasdale's eye.

'Edwards . . .'

'Yes, sir.'

'Emmott . . .'

'Sir . . .'

'Gower . . .'

'Sir . . .'

How did he do it? How could anyone look down with one eye and stare straight ahead with the other? It was impossible. I tried it. I looked down at my desk with my right eye, just like Mr Bleasdale, and tried to keep my left eye up. It was impossible.

But it wasn't. Mr Bleasdale could do it. Perhaps *all* Grammar School teachers could do it . . . Oh dear . . .

'Holdsworth . . .'

'Yes, sir.'

'Hopkinson . . .'

'Yes, sir . . .'

'Hopwood . . .'

'Sir.'

Oh dear. At High Moor Primary we used to get away with murder when the teacher wasn't looking. Especially in Miss Dixon's classes. Here we wouldn't be able to do anything – except work. Certainly with Mr Bleasdale 'cos he'd always be looking.

'Lightowler . . .'

'Yes, sir.'

Even Norbert Lightowler was behaving himself. And he was dressed smartly for once. Well, for him. He hadn't got a brand new blazer like everyone else – his mum couldn't afford it, but she'd managed to get hold of a second-hand one from somewhere. It was miles too big for him but Norbert didn't seem to mind. Norbert was the only other lad I knew in 1B. We'd been at High Moor together and everybody was surprised when he'd got into Grammar School – especially Norbert. His mum wasn't very pleased because it meant him staying on at school till he was sixteen. She'd have rather he left as soon as possible and get a job and bring some money in like the rest of his brothers and sisters. That's what my mum said anyway.

At Primary School I'd always found Norbert a bit of a nuisance, always telling me I was his best friend, forever hanging round trying to get into our gang. But today I was glad he was sitting next to me. At least I *knew* somebody, had somebody to talk to. Tony, my best friend, had come to the Grammar as well but he'd been put into 1 Alpha. I couldn't wait to ask him if *his* teacher could watch the class with one eye while he looked down with the other.

'McDougall . . .'

'Sir.'

'Mudd . . .'

'Sir.'

Mudd. Fancy having a name like that, Mudd. Everybody giggled and a few including me and Norbert looked round to see what he looked like. He was a big lad, probably the biggest in the class. I wouldn't be laughing at his name again.

'Thank you, gentlemen, you've got this next five years to get to know each other so I'd be grateful if I could have your undivided attention for the next few minutes.'

I turned back to the front as Mr Bleasdale carried on calling out our names, his right eye on the register, his left eye on us.

'Nunn . . .'

'Yes, sir.'

3

That was the *first* time I'd seen Mr Bleasdale. It was the last time our class would be so well behaved for him.

By the end of morning break on that first day I'd found out the truth. Or at least Norbert had. I was in the playground telling Tony about Mr Bleasdale's trick when Norbert came up to me. He'd already torn one of his blazer pockets.

'Hey, you'll never guess what I've just found out.'

'Shurrup a minute will you, I'm just telling Tony about Mr Bleasdale. Honest, Tony, he can look down and write with his one eye, and watch the class with his other. Both at the same time.'

I could tell Tony didn't believe me, the way he was looking.

'Honestly, it's true. It's a fantastic trick, isn't it, Norbert?'

Nobert wiped his nose with his sleeve and nodded.

'Yeah . . . It'd be even better if he could see out of the eye he's watching with.'

I looked at Norbert. He wiped his nose again, with his other sleeve this time.

'Y'what?'

'It's a glass eye. It's not real. It's made of glass . . .'

I sat at my desk staring at the glass eye. I still found it hard to believe he couldn't see me, even now, nine months later. It looked so real – except that it never blinked.

Norbert had no doubts – he was mucking about as usual and Bleasdale looked up just in time to see him flicking a paper pellet at David Holdsworth.

'I saw that, Lightowler. I'm not blind, you know. Get on with your revision. You got exams in three days.'

'Yes, sir.'

Norbert shoved his head into his Latin textbook and sniggered at the lads around him. When Bleasdale looked down – with his one eye – Norbert made a funny face at him, putting his fingers to his ears and waggling them, and sticking his tongue out. He's not bothered about school work and exams, Norbert. *I* had to do well or I'd be in big trouble with my mum. If I didn't do well – *very* well – not only would I be in big trouble but I wouldn't be allowed to go on the school trip to London to see the Festival of Britain.

Mr Bleasdale and Mr Melrose were organising it. It was a day trip and it was going to cost fifteen pounds. I was dead lucky to have my name down because when I'd asked my mum if I could go, she'd said no. In fact she'd said no, no, no!

'No, no, no! Where do you think I'm going to get fifteen pounds from? You must be living in cloud-cuckoo-land, young man.'

'We can pay in instalments, Mr Bleasdale says so.'

She gave me one of her looks.

'Oh, does he? Well you can tell Mr Bleasdale that I'm still paying for your school uniform in instalments, and your satchel, and your bike . . .'

That's when she saw the tear in my blazer.

'Just come here a minute.'

Oh no, it was that stupid Norbert's fault when he'd been trying to get ahead of me in the dinner queue. He'd got hold my pocket and swung me round. That's how it had ripped. Stupid idiot.

'Look at your new blazer. What on earth have you been up to?'

5

I don't know why she keeps calling it my 'new' blazer. I got it last September.

'That's a brand new blazer – look at your pocket. Take it off!'

I tried to tell her it was Norbert's fault but she wouldn't listen. She just yanked the blazer off my back and got her sewing machine out. She's paying for that in instalments too.

'You're lucky it's torn on the seam.'

I didn't say anything else about the school trip to London. I didn't dare.

'And don't you dare talk to me about school trips to London . . .'

I didn't have to. I was dead lucky. I got given the money. All fifteen pounds. In fact I had over fifteen pounds in my Post Office Saving Book. Sixteen pounds, four and fourpence to be exact. I'd put the one pound four and fourpence in last Saturday. One pound from my Auntie Doreen for clearing out her garden shed, and four and fourpence for the empty Guinness and Lucozade bottles I'd found in there. I'd taken them to the corner off-licence on my way to Youth Club. My mum had told me off for taking the one pound.

'It's far too much. Your Auntie Doreen can't afford that kind of money. How long did it take you to clean the shed out?'

'Nearly an hour! I was late for Youth Club.'

It hadn't really taken me that long. I was there for the best part of an hour but I'd spend a lot of the time looking at these old magazines. They were called 'National Geo-something' and they were ever so interesting. Pictures of natives with darts through their lips, that sort of thing. I'd asked my Auntie Doreen if I could have them but she wouldn't let me.

'No, they belonged to your Uncle Norman and it wouldn't be right to give them away. Put them back in the shed.'

So back they'd gone under the old deckchairs and watering-cans and paint pots. And fishing tackle! Ooh, I'd love to have had a go with that fishing tackle. I'd asked my Auntie Doreen even though I knew what she'd say.

'No, it wouldn't be right, it were your Uncle Norman's.'

I don't know how long ago my Uncle Norman had died – I mean I'd never even known him – but it seemed daft to me shoving all these good things to the back of the shed.

'Nearly an hour! A pound for less than an hour! That's more than I get from Mrs Jerome.'

My mum goes cleaning for Mrs Jerome three mornings a week. It's a great big house on the other side of the park. It's where the rich people live. They've got a treehouse in their garden and Mrs Jerome lets me play in it sometimes. She's ever so nice. It's thanks to her I'm going on the school trip because she gave me the money.

I'd been over there playing in the treehouse one Saturday morning while my mum was cleaning and Mrs Jerome had brought out some orange squash and some chocolate biscuits for me. Not just on one side. Chocolate on both sides. They were lovely. I think Mrs Jerome likes me coming to play in the treehouse because all her children are grown-up. Except one, he got killed in the war. Anyway she'd started asking me how I was enjoying Grammar School and I'd said all right and what did I want to be when I grew up and I'd said I didn't know and who was my favourite film star and so

7

on. And then she'd asked me what was happening in the school holidays, was I going anywhere? And I'd told her we'd probably be doing the same as usual, going on the odd day trip to Morecambe and Scarborough with my mum and my Auntie Doreen and she'd said she and Mr Jerome would be doing the same as usual, a cruise to the Canary Islands. She'd said that I could play in the treehouse while she was away.

'Actually, I'm ever so excited because Mr Jerome has arranged for us to stop off in London for a few days to visit the Festival of Britain.'

And I'd told her about the school trip to London to see the Festival of Britain too, and how it cost fifteen pounds and how I couldn't go because my mum couldn't afford it.

Well, the following Tuesday I'd come home from school and my mum was sitting at the kitchen table holding a small book. She'd looked as though she'd been crying.

'What's the matter, Mum? Are you all right?'

She hadn't said anything, she'd just given me the little book. It was a Post Office Savings Book. I'd opened it and it had my name written inside and there was fifteen pounds in the account.

I'd looked at my mum and I couldn't tell whether she was pleased or cross.

'You're not going to London if you do badly in your exams. If you don't do well – very well – that money's going straight back to Mrs Jerome!'

I stared at my Latin textbook.

'Amo, Amas, Amat . . .'

It was all Greek to me. The bell went for home-time and everybody started packing up.

Bleasdale was tapping on his desk to get our attention. Norbert was practically out of the door.

'One minute, gentlemen, and that includes you, Light-owler – homework!'

Everybody groaned. I had tons already. French revision, an English essay, Maths.

'I'm not setting any homework tonight . . .'

Everybody cheered.

'But I want you to do some extensive revision.'

Everybody groaned again.

'I shall be giving you a written vocabulary test tomorrow . . .'

More groans.

'It'll be your last test before the exams. Now go home, you horrible lot, and do some work!'

We piled out into the corridor and the headmaster hit Norbert on the side of his head and told him to stop running. He and a few others were off to play cricket in the schoolyard.

'Who's coming? It's Yorkshire against Lancashire. I'm Freddie Truman. And when I'm batting I'm Willie Watson.'

I didn't want to play cricket. I wanted to get on with my revision. I wanted to go to London. Anyway I never got a chance to bat. By the time it came to my turn we usually got kicked out by the caretaker.

I don't know why I went to play in the treehouse. It's not even on my way home. But I started walking with David Holdsworth and he goes that way through the park. Maybe

I wanted to show off to him, I don't know, but that's what I did. I pointed to it as we went up the hill past Mrs Jerome's.

'You see that treehouse. Up there. I'm allowed to play in it.'

He looked at it. It's about fifteen feet up in a big syca-more tree.

'I bet you wish you were.'

'I am. Honest.'

I couldn't stop myself from smiling and because I was smiling he thought I was lying. I soon showed him I wasn't. I led the way up the ladder.

After we'd been playing for about a quarter of an hour I decided it was time to go.

'I've got to go soon. I've got to get on with my revision.'

David was pretending to be a commando in Korea.

'Pow, pow! Oh, don't go yet. It's great up here. Pow, pow!'

I wish we had gone. We wouldn't have been there when Norbert came past. It was David who saw him first, running up the hill.

'Look, there's Norbert. He must've got kicked out by the caretaker. Pow, pow! You're dead, Norbert.'

He looked round to see where the voice had come from.

'What are you doing up there? I'm coming up.'

I tried to stop him. I wanted to get home. Besides, even though *I* was allowed to play in the treehouse I didn't think Mrs Jerome would like it if half the school turned up. It was a good job she was away.

'No, Norbert, we're going now.'

But he was halfway up the ladder.

'Oh in't it great. Don't tell any of the other lads, we'll keep it for ourselves.'

Keep it for ourselves. He had some cheek, did Norbert.

'*I'm* the only one allowed to play here. I know the owner. Now come on, get down!'

He didn't get down. He came in.

'Hey, you'll never guess what I've found . . .'

He started rummaging under his jumper.

'These were in the dustbin we used as a wicket – look!'

He held out some sheets of paper with purple writing on it but I couldn't tell what they said because the writing was backwards.

'It's rubbish this, all the writing's backwards.'

'It is not rubbish, they're our exam papers. These are the stencils that Mrs Smylie runs all the copies off . . .'

Mrs Smylie's the school secretary.

' . . . These are the questions we'll be getting. Look, 1B – Summer Term.'

Holdsworth grabbed one of the papers. We looked at it. Norbert was right. It was 1B Summer Term spelt backwards.

'Yeah, look – this is geography backwards.'

He knelt down and started going through the questions, working out what they said. Norbert knelt down opposite him.

'They're all here. English, Latin, French, Religious Instruction.'

They started reading the questions out loud . . . I didn't want to hear them. I didn't want to cheat. I wanted to do well in my exams. I wanted to go to The Festival of Britain but I didn't want to cheat.

'Stop. You mustn't, it's not right . . .'

11

I tried to get the papers before either of them could read any more. I was going to tear them up and throw them away but Norbert stopped me.

I don't think he meant to push me that hard. Fifteen feet doesn't sound very high, but it is when you're falling out of a treehouse.

I didn't do much that summer. There's not much you can do when you've broken both your legs. I didn't do the exams either. I couldn't with my right arm in plaster. My mum made me go to school though. She said there was no reason why I couldn't sit and read while the others did their exams. But I didn't do much reading. I spent most of the time staring at Bleasdale's glass eye ... Thinking about the school trip I wouldn't be going on.

My mum used the fifteen pounds to mend the treehouse.

THE SECOND PRIZE

I could hear my mum upstairs bustling about, getting herself
ready, asking my Auntie Doreen which hat she should wear.

'What do you think, Doreen, the black velvet I wore to
Matty's funeral or the royal blue with the cherries? Which
looks most suitable?'

I heard my Auntie Doreen thinking. You could always
hear her when she was thinking – she sucked in her breath
and it made her false teeth rattle.

'It's not a funeral we're going to, is it? It's a prize-giving.
I'd wear the royal blue.'

My mum couldn't make her mind up.

'I don't know ... the black velvet's very stylish and it
goes with my two-piece ... mind you, so does the royal
blue ... I don't know. Maybe I shouldn't wear a hat. I don't
want to be overdressed, do I? You're not wearing a hat.'

I could hear my Auntie Doreen sighing now. It's funny
how her teeth didn't rattle when she breathed out, only when
she breathed in.

'Well, whatever you do, you'd better do it fast or we're
going to be late!'

I was sitting at the top of the stairs listening, my stomach
churning. My stomach seemed to have been churning for the
last two weeks, ever since I'd heard I'd won the second prize.
I'd been ready for ages. I was wearing my best suit, the one

my mum had got in the sale at Lewis' in Leeds, and this was only the second time I'd worn it. The first time was at my Uncle Matty's funeral and I'd got into trouble with my mum at the tea afterwards. It had been my Auntie Winnie's fault, Uncle Matty's wife. She hadn't seen me for years and she'd come rolling over towards me just as I was about to eat another cream horn. I'd been really careful eating the first one because my mum had warned me not to spill *anything* on my new suit. When I saw Auntie Winnie coming towards me I was more worried she was going to spill her glass of sherry over me and I started backing away.

'Eeh, is that our Freda's lad? I'd never have recognised you . . .' And the next thing I knew she was putting her arms round me and giving me a big hug and a kiss.

It was horrible. It wasn't just the smell of the sherry on her breath. She had a wart on her upper lip with long hairs growing out of it and I could feel it. I could feel something else too – the cream horn being squashed onto my chest. Onto my new suit. While she was hugging and kissing me and saying how proud Uncle Matty would have been to see me grow into such a fine young man she finished off the sherry and asked me to get her another one.

My mum had gone mad when she saw the state of my new suit. She'd taken me straight into the bathroom.

'Brand new, and you have to go and get cream all over it! I could cheerfully throttle you!'

'It wasn't my fault, Mum . . .' And I'd explained how Auntie Winnie had hugged me and squashed the cream horn.

She didn't say much. She just rubbed away with a flannel and muttered something about Winnie and her drinking and something about driving Matty to an early grave. My mum

14

and Auntie Winnie didn't get on that well. That's why we hardly ever saw them.

Anyway it had come back from the dry-cleaners looking as good as new – well it was new, I'd only worn it the once – and I sat at the top of the stairs waiting to set off for the prize-giving, my stomach churning.

The doorbell rang and I heard my mum going into a panic.

'Ooh, that'll be the taxi and I'm nowhere ready. If that's the taxi, love, tell him I'll be a couple of minutes.'

I went downstairs to answer the door. I wouldn't have minded if she took another couple of hours, I was dreading the whole thing. It *was* the taxi.

'My mum's not ready yet, she'll be a few minutes.'

It was the same driver who'd taken us to the station when we'd gone to Uncle Matty's funeral.

'Well, she booked me for quarter-to, I'll have to charge waiting time. Can I use your lavatory?'

'Yeah, it's out the back.'

I showed him to the toilet and went back in to hurry my mum up. Not that I wanted to get there quickly – I wished we didn't have to go at all – but I didn't want my mum to get charged too much waiting time.

'It's only just quarter-to now, he was early. Are my seams straight, Doreen?'

Auntie Doreen checked my mum's stockings and my mum checked my Auntie Doreen's stockings, then my mum straightened my tie, brushed the dandruff off my jacket and off we went downstairs. They were both wearing hats – my mum had the royal blue on and Auntie Doreen was wearing

15

the black velvet. My mum slammed the front door shut and was looking in her handbag for her keys.

'Hey Doreen, I hope we're not overdressed.'

My Auntie Doreen was looking in her powder compact, dabbing her nose and making funny in and out movements with her lips.

'I don't think so. It's not every day one of the family is summoned to the Town Hall to be presented with a prize, is it?'

They both smiled at me and my Auntie Doreen kissed me on the cheek. I felt terrible. If they only knew the truth.

As she was double-locking the front door my mum started going on about keeping my best suit clean.

'And don't you spill *anything* on that suit. We don't want a repeat of last time.'

I was just about to tell her for the umpteenth time that it wasn't my fault but my Auntie Doreen did it for me.

'Leave him alone, Freda. You can't blame him. You know what our Winnie's like when she's had a drink. Now come on, let's not keep this taxi waiting any longer.'

And we set off down the path.

We'd just got into the car when my Auntie Doreen noticed that there was no driver.

'Hang on – where's the driver?'

I explained that he'd asked to use the toilet.

'He's probably still out there, Mum. You've locked him out the back!'

She sighed and got the keys back out of her handbag.

'And he wants to charge me waiting time. I'll charge him toilet time . . .!'

16

She scurried off up the path and my Auntie Doreen smiled at me.

'Are you excited?'

I looked at her. If only she knew how I really felt. Should I tell her the truth?

'Auntie Doreen . . .?'

'Yes, love?'

It'd be easier to tell her than my mum. She'd get rid of the taxi and we'd go back into the house. I'd go upstairs to my bedroom while she and my mum would go into the kitchen. My Auntie Doreen would make her a cup of tea and gently tell her the truth . . . And I'd sit at the top of the stairs trying to listen . . . No I wouldn't, I wouldn't *want* to listen, I wouldn't want to hear. I'd lie on my bed and wait . . . And after a while, after Auntie Doreen had gone home, my mum would come up and her eyes would be all red and I'd still be lying on the bed and she'd tell me not to lie on the bed in my best suit and I'd look at her . . . at her red eyes and her disappointed face . . . and I'd wish I'd never said anything.

'Yes, love?'

I saw the taxi driver coming down the path with my mum.

'It's the same driver who took us to the station when we went to Uncle Matty's funeral.'

It was all I could think of saying. I couldn't tell her the truth. Not with my mum all dressed up in her royal blue hat and everything, so proud of me and excited. How could I tell her that it shouldn't be me getting this prize? The driver was laughing to himself as he got in the car.

'I tell you, that's a first . . . Wait till I tell the wife. I hope you're not catching a train?'

My mum wasn't laughing. She put on her posh voice.

'No, we're going to the Town Hall. Main entrance.'

The driver started the engine. Oh, the way she said it in that stupid voice. 'We're going to the Town Hall. Main entrance.' And why did she have to waggle her head like that? And smile as if she had a piece of lemon in her mouth? Knowing that I shouldn't even be getting this prize made it even worse. If only she hadn't had to go away to Blackpool none of this would have happened.

My mum and my Auntie Doreen do voluntary work for the old folk. I don't know how old these old folk are because my mum and my Auntie Doreen aren't young. Anyway, not long after I'd started at the grammar school they took the old folk on an outing to Blackpool to see the illuminations which meant my mum staying away. So she arranged for me to sleep the night with Mr and Mrs Carpenter at number 23. I often went to their house if my mum was going to be late back from work or anything like that but this was the first time I'd gone to stay all night.

'You sure you don't mind? I can try and get someone else to go to Blackpool in my place.'

I didn't mind.

'No, I'll be all right.'

I liked going to Mr and Mrs Carpenter's. They're ever so kind. I think they like me coming because they don't have any children. They had a son once called David but he died when he was a baby. He came too early or something. Mr Carpenter has this fantastic collection of tin soldiers

18

and he lets me play with them. I think they're quite valuable.

'Well, it's only for one night. Are you sure you'll be OK?'

'Yes!'

Oh, my mum didn't half go on sometimes. I wouldn't have minded if she stayed away a bit longer, but I didn't say that in case it upset her.

'I'll be all right. Honest.'

I think my mum thought I was being brave because she spoke in the same sort of voice she put on when I had to have an injection at the doctor's.

'Well, I'll take your things round to Mrs Carpenter's in the morning before we set off for Blackpool and you go straight there after school. You'll be all right.'

I didn't go straight there after school because Mr Carpenter met me and took me into town for an ice cream and then we went to Dyson's toy shop and he said I could choose anything I wanted up to two pounds. I didn't like to at first because I thought my mum might be cross but he said it was his treat and nothing to do with anybody else and I should choose what I wanted.

'But no more than two pound, mind, and don't say anything to Mrs Carpenter about having an ice cream or you'll get me into trouble. We've got a big tea waiting at home.'

I chose a box of coloured pencils at first because I'd got art homework to do but Mr Carpenter told me to choose something else.

'I've got a load of crayons at home, I'll give you some. Treat yourself to something you really fancy.'

What I'd really wanted was this commando that had a string in its back and when you pulled it said different orders like 'Enemy at one o'clock' and 'Do you surrender?' and other things. It was great. It cost one pound nineteen and eleven and I put the penny change in the box for deaf children. We got back at about half past five and Mrs Carpenter must have known we'd be going into town because she wasn't surprised how late we were.

'Now – are you hungry?'

I looked at Mr Carpenter. I couldn't say, 'No, I've just had a big ice cream.' Luckily Mrs Carpenter carried on talking.

'Because we can either eat now or you can do your homework first.'

'I'd like to get my homework done, Mrs Carpenter.'

'Good idea. Now, we've got roast chicken for tea. Do you like chicken?'

I *loved* chicken. We only have it at Christmas and Easter.

'I *love* chicken.'

Mr Carpenter got a whole load of coloured pencils out of a drawer and gave them to me.

'Can I keep all these?'

'Aye, 'course you can. Now what's this art you have to do?

I told him the choice Mr Clegg the art teacher had given us.

'We have to draw either a street scene or a woodland scene. I'm going to do a street scene.'

So he cleared a space at the table for me and sat down to read his paper while Mrs Carpenter went into the kitchen to finish off her ironing.

20

I started my picture using the coloured pencils Mr Carpenter had given me. I drew a zebra crossing. Then I drew a car and a boy and a girl waiting to cross. I'm not very good at drawing – I never have been – and I suddenly realised Mr Carpenter was standing behind me, watching. I felt a bit embarrassed.

'It's not very good, is it?'

He smiled.

'Don't use your crayons straight off. Do it lightly in pencil to start, then you can rub it out and change it if you want. Look.'

He got himself a chair, sat down beside me and started drawing on a new piece of paper. He copied what I'd done, the zebra crossing, the car, the boy and girl, but in pencil like he said. He was a good drawer.

'Now, what else do you want, couple of shops? Someone on a bike maybe? I know, let's have a police car.'

Mrs Carpenter came in from the kitchen and when she realised what he was doing she told him off.

'Hey, he's supposed to be doing that homework, Denzil, not you.'

'I'm just giving the lad a bit of a hand, that's all. He's got the hard work to do, he's got to colour it all in.'

Mr Carpenter went back to his paper and I started colouring. It took me ages. There were lots of people in it now, a lady pushing a pram, a couple of the old folk going into a Post Office (that was my idea), and a boy on roller skates. And there was a Woolworth's and a dry-cleaner's, and a National Provincial Bank. When I'd finished, it was a really good picture. The best I'd ever done. Well I knew I hadn't done it but like Mr Carpenter said, I'd done the hard work, I'd done all the colouring. Anyway I didn't think it mattered. As long as Norbert Lightowler didn't see it. We'd been at High Moor Primary together before we'd gone to the grammar school and he knew I wasn't good at art. And it *wouldn't* have mattered if Mr Clegg hadn't shown it to the headmaster . . .

Art is the last lesson we have on a Thursday morning and when the dinner bell went Mr Clegg told us to leave our homework on his desk on the way out.

'And make sure you've put your name on the back, otherwise I'll not know which of these works of art belongs to which genius. Lightowler, name on the back, lad.'

Norbert came back and signed his picture. Mr Carpenter had rolled mine up and put a rubber band round it which was good because it meant nobody could see it. Norbert had wanted to have a look but I'd told him I couldn't be bothered to unroll it.

'I bet it's not as good as mine.'

Norbert took his out of a folder to show me and David Holdsworth.

'Look at that. A Woodland Scene by Norbert Lightowler. Good, innit?'

It was quite good. A bit messy but then Norbert's work always is. And he'd put in monkeys and tigers. Holdsworth started laughing.

'You don't get tigers and monkeys in a wood, that's more like a jungle scene.'

Norbert had just sniffed and wiped his nose on the back of his sleeve.

'Well, there are monkeys and tigers in *this* wood, so tough!' And he put it back in his folder.

As Norbert was writing his name I put my picture on Mr Clegg's desk. I'd signed it on the back the night before. We went off into the playground and I didn't think much more about it.

The next time we had art Mr Clegg picked out a few of the pictures and told us what was right and what was wrong.

'You see, look at Hopkinson's – this chap here is taller than the Belisha beacon.'

Everybody laughed and Hopkinson went all red. He's always going red.

'Now Lightowler's isn't bad at all . . .'

Everybody turned round and looked at Norbert. He licked his thumb and wiped it on his chest, all cocky.

'It's a bit messy,' – everybody laughed and Norbert screwed up his nose – 'but the perspective is good. Mind you, Lightowler, I did say a woodland scene, not a jungle scene.'

We all laughed again and that was it. We went on to something else. I was a bit annoyed. My picture was much better than Norbert's but Mr Clegg never mentioned it. Not then anyway. He did a few weeks later. Well, he didn't, the headmaster did.

We were in the middle of a Latin lesson with Mr Bleasdale when the headmaster and Mr Clegg came in. The headmaster whispered something to Bleasdale then all three looked at the class. I thought they were looking at me . . . They were! Bleasdale told me to stand up. I didn't know what was going on. The headmaster took a pace forward and the whole class was staring at me. I couldn't think what I'd done wrong.

'This boy has brought great honour to the school.'

I couldn't think what I'd done right.

'Some weeks ago you were set some work by Mr Clegg. You were asked to draw a street scene. One of these drawings was quite outstanding and Mr Clegg showed it to me . . .'

I could feel myself going red. My legs felt like jelly.

' . . . and I agreed with him. It was outstanding and I sent this drawing up to London to be considered in this year's National Road Safety Art Competition . . .'

My heart was pounding. I tried to swallow but my mouth had gone all dry.

'I am delighted to say that this drawing has won a Regional second prize in the under-12 category, which means that this lad has come second in the whole county.'

Mr Clegg started clapping and the headmaster joined in, then Bleasdale and then the whole class. I thought I was going to be sick. My stomach started to churn . . .

It was churning now in the back of the taxi.

I looked out of the window. We were on the main road heading for the city centre. The driver was tapping his fingers on the steering wheel, waiting for the lights to change.

'So, what's going on at the Town Hall today?'

My mum looked at me. She put on her posh voice again. She put it on every time she told someone.

'The National Road Safety Art Competition. Regional prize-giving. My son's won second prize in the under-12s. Second in the whole county!'

I was sitting in the middle, between my mum and my Auntie Doreen, and I could see the driver looking at me in his mirror. He smiled.

'Second in the whole county, eh? You must be a good artist.'

I just about managed to smile back.

'Not bad.'

'Not bad? You must be a lot better than "not bad" to come second in the whole county. He's too modest, your young lad.'

My mum put her arm through mine. We turned right into Delius Street. We were nearly at the Town Hall.

'Well, that's the funny thing. Art has never been his strong point, has it, love . . .?'

I shook my head.

'But he's just started at the grammar school and his new art teacher must have brought out hidden talents, eh love?'

I nodded. I felt sick. My mum carried on chatting to the driver.

'I haven't seen it yet, you know. Me and my sister were away in Blackpool when he did it. We'll be seeing it for the first time today. We're ever so proud of him, aren't we, Doreen?'

My Auntie Doreen took hold of my other arm and I sat between them as they held me close.

Yes, they were so proud of me. Everybody was so proud of me. Mr Clegg, the headmaster, my mum, my Auntie Doreen. That's why I hadn't said anything right at the start. I'd planned to go to the headmaster the day after he'd told me in class, explain to him what had happened, *how* it had happened, but he announced it in assembly. I'd even had to go up on the stage and shake his hand while the whole school applauded.

We pulled up outside the Town Hall. We were there. While my mum was paying him the driver asked me what the prize was.

'Fifteen pounds in National Savings stamps.'

He nodded and said very nice and told my mum he wouldn't be charging waiting time.

'I should think not, we were waiting for you.' And we went up the steps into the Town Hall.

There were lots of other prize-winners going in, girls as well as boys, and most had their mums and dads with them. Some had their grandparents. On the invitation it had said we were allowed 'four per family'. I never knew my grandma – she died when I was two – and my grandad died a couple of years ago. My mum had invited Mr and Mrs Carpenter but thank goodness they couldn't come, they'd had to go to a wedding in Doncaster. When my mum had told them about me coming second Mr Carpenter didn't ask me if it was for the picture I'd done at his house – and I didn't tell him. He must have known, though. He knew I wasn't good enough to win a prize.

We were walking through this big entrance hall with stone pillars and marble floors. Quite a few of the prize-winners were wearing their school uniforms but my mum had wanted me to wear my best suit. Norbert Lightowler had torn my blazer trying to get ahead of me in the dinner queue and even though my mum had mended it, it was still a bit scruffy.

Everybody was talking in whispers and our footsteps echoed everywhere. It reminded me of when we went into the church at Uncle Matty's funeral. At the far end a com-missionaire was directing people.

'National Road Safety – main chamber at the top of the stairs. Main chamber at the top of the stairs for the National Road Safety prize-giving.'

26

My stomach churned even more when I heard him saying 'prize-giving'. Soon I was going to be presented with a prize that I had no right to. A prize for something I hadn't done. I felt sick. I had to go to the toilet. I whispered to my mum.

'All right, love, we'll ask at the top of the stairs.'

We went up this wide staircase and on the walls on either side were old-fashioned pictures of old men. This lad's mother was telling him that they were portraits of previous Lord Mayors and that maybe one day his portrait would be up there and they both laughed. She talked loudly so that everybody around could hear and she put on a posh voice like my mum, only I think she *was* posh because he called her 'mummy' not 'mum' and I heard her saying how bad the traffic had been coming from Harrogate and Harrogate's a very posh place.

Another commissionaire explained where the toilets were and my mum told me to wait for her and Auntie Doreen outside the ladies and I went into the gents. There was nobody in there, thank goodness. I just wanted to be on my own for a minute. I felt terrible. All the other winners were smiling and laughing and were so excited. I felt like a cheat. I was a cheat. *I* hadn't won the second prize, Mr Carpenter had. I didn't want this rotten prize but what could I do about it? I'd been awarded it and I'd have to accept it. Thank goodness I hadn't won *first* prize otherwise I would have had to go to London. All the top Regional winners had to go for the National prize-giving. At least after today it'd all be over with. I splashed some water on my face, had a drink and went to meet my mum. I had to use my hanky to dry myself because there was no towel.

To get into the main chamber we had to show our invitation to the commissionaire and my mum got into a panic because she thought she'd forgotten it. She couldn't find it in her handbag.

'Eh, Doreen, I think I left it on the hall table when I was looking for the camera . . .'

I was hoping she wouldn't find it. Auntie Doreen was helping her look.

'Freda, I said "Have you got the invitation?" Twice I reminded you.'

'I know, I know!'

My mum was getting into a right state and I felt sorry for her. But I felt more sorry for myself and I was praying like mad.

'Please God, don't let her find it, don't let her find it, then they won't let us in and we can go home and I won't get presented with the prize.'

My mum didn't find it. But we didn't go home.

'You're all right . . .' The commissionaire winked at me. 'He looks like an honest lad. We don't want him going home without his prize, do we?'

No, I wanted to shout, I'm not an honest lad, I didn't do the picture, Mr Carpenter did it and I *do* want to go home without my prize. But I just said thank you and we went into the main chamber.

The seats were in rows with a gangway down the middle. My mum wanted to be near the front so she could get a good photo of me receiving my prize so we sat in the third row. The main chamber was ever so big and around the room were more portraits of previous Lord Mayors. On the wall facing us, in gold lettering, were the names

28

of every Lord Mayor since 1874 and there was a scroll of honour like we've got at school with a list of people who had been killed in both world wars. At the front was a stage with three pictures on easels marked first, second and third. There was a little lad in front of us getting all excited because one of them was his and his mum and dad told him to calm down. At the side on the floor were all the winning pictures stacked up. I sat between my mum and my Auntie Doreen reading the names of the Lord Mayors, wishing the whole thing was over.

I could hear the lady from Harrogate in the row behind.

'Yes, Jeremy's won first prize in the under-12s. Of course what he's most excited about is the trip to London.'

My mum smiled at me and squeezed my hand. I suppose she thought I was wishing I'd come first so that I'd be going to London. I smiled back and started reading the names of the people who'd been killed in the First World War.

'Albert Bartholomew ... Douglas Briggs ... Maurice Clarkson ...'

Then it started, the prize-giving.

One of the officials blew into a microphone and a man from London welcomed everybody and said the standard had been extremely high and that the judges had found it extremely difficult to decide on the three winners in each category and he was extremely pleased to introduce the editor of the *Yorkshire Post* to present the prizes. Then he asked for the under-10 winners to come up on the stage.

They stood in front of their own easel and as their name was called out and the editor presented the prizes everybody clapped. The little lad who'd got excited was Graham Duck-worth from Otley and he'd come third. The lady from

Harrogate tapped my mum on the shoulder and asked if she'd mind taking her hat off because people behind couldn't see. My mum went a bit red and looked quite cross but she and my Auntie Doreen took them off and put them under their seats. The under-10 pictures were taken away and the under-11s were called up. As they were going up on the stage their pictures were put on the easels. They were really good and everybody clapped again as each name was called out.

Then it was my turn.

'Can I have the winners from the under-12 category, please?'

My mum and my Auntie Doreen turned towards me with great big grins on their faces. I stood up and slowly squeezed past the other people sitting in our row. A man at the end patted me on the back and said 'Well done, lad.' Jeremy from Harrogate was already walking up the gangway and I followed him. We watched them take away the under-11 pictures and went on the stage and stood in front of our easels. The third winner was a tall lad with ginger hair and a birthmark on his cheek who did a thumbs-up to the audience. I stared ahead, trying not to look at my mum, but out of the corner of my eye I saw her taking a photo. There was a flash and when I looked at her she signalled at me to smile. I could hear them behind me putting our pictures on the easels but I didn't look round. I didn't want to see mine. I just kept on looking at the back of the room. I concentrated on this coat of arms above the door. I felt as if I was going to cry. How had I got myself into this mess? Why hadn't I told the truth right at the beginning? I could hear the man from London tapping the microphone.

'And now, ladies and gentlemen, boys and girls, we

come to the under-12 category. Once again the standard has been extremely high and third place is awarded to Trevor Hainsworth from Driffield.'

Everybody clapped him as he got his prize and he did another thumbs-up to the audience.

'And the second prize goes to . . .' And as I heard my name being called out I felt a pain in my stomach and to stop myself from bursting into tears I just made myself keep looking at the coat of arms at the back. It was a blue and red and gold shield and standing on their hind legs on either side of the shield were a golden stag and a silver ram and on top of the shield was a knight's helmet. That was in gold too. Then the editor was shaking my hand.

'Congratulations. Well done, young man.'

I think I said 'thank you', I can't remember now. I could hear my mum saying 'smile' and there was another flash but I didn't look at her. I couldn't.

'And the first prize in the under-12s goes to Jeremy Collins from Harrogate for this magnificent drawing . . .'

Underneath the coat of arms in gold lettering was written 'Honesty – Toil – Honour'.

'And of course Jeremy will go forward and represent this county at the National awards early next year.'

'Honesty – Toil – Honour.' I kept looking at the coat of arms as Jeremy got his prize from the editor. Twenty-five pounds in National Savings stamps. 'Honesty – Toil – Honour.'

Nobody heard me at first because of all the clapping and when it died down I said it again, quietly. The man from London wasn't sure if he'd heard me properly.

'What did you say?'

'It's not my picture. I didn't do it.'

I don't think most people in the audience knew what was going on because I said it so softly but they knew something was wrong because they started whispering to each other and all the officials on the stage were in a huddle. I could hear them saying that these were the winning pictures and that they were definitely in the right order. One of them took me on one side.

'What are you talking about, lad?'

'My picture – it's not mine. I didn't do it!'

And I turned round and pointed.

And it wasn't mine. I mean it wasn't the one Mr Carpenter did. It was a different picture altogether. It wasn't as good as Mr Carpenter's. I could see Jeremy staring at me. He looked strange, sort of frightened.

Then I saw why – Mr Carpenter's picture was on *his* easel. Mr Carpenter had won first prize, not Jeremy – but he hadn't said anything. The man from London was tapping the microphone again.

'I'm sorry, ladies and gentlemen, we seem to have a little confusion. If you could . . . er . . . bear with us for a moment we'd be most grateful. Thank you.'

Then he turned back to me.

'Are any of these drawings yours?'

The tall lad with ginger hair got quite cross.

'Well, he didn't do this one. It's mine!'

The audience was getting fidgety. I couldn't understand why Jeremy hadn't said anything yet but I suppose it was still dawning on him that he hadn't won the first prize after all. He looked stunned. I felt happier than I had done for weeks.

32

'No, I didn't do any of these.'

I knew that when it came round to Jeremy telling them that he hadn't done the picture on his easel either, they'd probably take the frame off to check and they'd see my name on the back. I didn't care. I'd tell them the truth. But they didn't check. Jeremy didn't say anything and they gave him first prize.

I don't know how he could accept a prize for something he hadn't done. I couldn't.

THE PIGEON

PART ONE

It was on the Thursday, during Latin with Mr Bleasdale, that
Arthur Boocock sent the note round. Three days after the
new boy had started. Latin's the last lesson before our dinner
break and we were doing translation while Bleasdale was
marking. We always muck about in his lessons 'cos you can
with his glass eye. You just have to make sure that his good
eye is looking down. Duggie Bashforth read the note, checked
that only the glass eye was looking, nodded at Arthur
Boocock, and passed it on. Kenny Spencer read it, nodded
at Arthur and gave it to Duncan Cawthra. Cawthra read it,
gave Arthur a nod and passed it to David Holdsworth. I
wondered what it said. Usually it was something to try and
make you laugh and get you into trouble. Or sometimes we
played 'the grot', when we passed anything round, somebody's cap or an exercise book, anything, and you had to
get rid of it before the bell went. Once it was a dead mouse
that Norbert had found down by the Mucky Beck. The
Mucky Beck is a small stream in Horton Woods. It's great
for frogspawn. Well it used to be. My mum doesn't let me
go there any more. Not since that lad from Galsworthy Road
Secondary Modern had got attacked. She'd read it in my
Auntie Doreen's paper.

'I don't want you playing down Horton Woods any

more, 'specially near the Mucky Beck. A lad from Galsworthy Road's been assaulted down there.'

She gave the paper to my Auntie Doreen and pointed to the bit she'd been reading.

'But I like playing down there. Mucky Beck's great for frogspawn.'

'You're not to go, I'm telling you. It's dangerous.'

What was my mum talking about? The Mucky Beck's only about six inches deep. My Auntie Doreen tutted to herself and gave the paper back to my mum.

'I don't know what the world's coming to, I really don't.'

'How can it be dangerous? Mucky Beck's only about six inches deep.'

'I don't want you going there, do you hear? A lad's been assaulted.'

I wasn't sure what she meant. What's 'a salted'? And why was it in the paper? I knew it was bad. My mum had her serious face on and whenever my Auntie Doreen reads something in the newspaper and says 'I don't know what the world is coming to', I know it's bad.

'What's a salted?'

My mum looked at my Auntie Doreen.

'He was attacked. A man attacked him. That's what it means.'

'Why?'

They looked at each other again, the way they look when they don't want to tell me something. They're always doing that. They weren't telling me the truth. They think I can't tell but I can.

'Why did he attack him? Was he a madman?'

He must have been mad to attack a Galsworthy Road

36

lad. Galsworthy Road Secondary Modern is where you go if you don't pass your scholarship to the Grammar and they're tough. I've heard some of them carry knives and things. I don't know if it's true but I wouldn't like to get into a fight with one of 'em. My Auntie Doreen got hold of my hand.

'Listen, love, this man was a bit sick in the head. There are people like that. That's why you must never go off with strangers. Do you understand?'

What was my Auntie Doreen talking about? I know all about strangers. My mum's always telling me. And we had a talk at school about it with Reverend Dutton, our scripture teacher. 'Course I wouldn't go off with a stranger. I'm not stupid. Anyway what's going off with strangers got to do with having a fight with someone? I bet the Galsworthy Road lad had cheeked him off or something – they're always getting into trouble.

''Course I wouldn't go off with a stranger. I didn't go with that bloke in the park who asked me if I wanted an ice cream, did I?'

It had happened in the Easter holidays. We'd all taken some bottles back to the shop, Tony, me and Norbert, and we'd gone to the park to spend our money at the fair. After I'd spent all mine, mostly on the slot machines and one go on the rifle range, I'd wandered around on my own for a bit while Tony and Norbert were on the dodgems.

I'd gone over to the waltzer and while I was watching and thinking that there was no way that *I'd* go on it – it goes at about a hundred miles an hour – this bloke had started talking to me.

'It's dead good, the waltzer. Best thing at fair.'

I'd told him it was too fast, that I wouldn't dare and that I hadn't got any money anyway.

'I'll pay for yer, young 'un, I've got tons o' money.'

I'd watched it whirling round and round. If it had been the dodgems I might have gone – I love the dodgems – but I didn't fancy the waltzer.

'No thanks.'

'Do you want an ice cream? I'll buy you one.'

That's when I'd realised he was a stranger. I'd remembered everything my mum had told me.

'No! And if you don't leave me alone I'm gonna tell a policeman.'

The man had just shrugged and sniffed and wandered off. Then I'd felt bad. Maybe he was just being friendly, nice. Norbert said I should have gone on.

'I would have. Free ride. And free ice cream. I'd have said yes.'

Yeah, Norbert would have. He's stupid. He doesn't realise about strangers. I don't think his mum and dad have told him properly. I don't think they're bothered. They never know where he goes and what he's up to. If he wants to go to the pictures and it's an 'A' he gets a stranger to take him in. He just goes up to any bloke who comes along and says 'Can you take us in, mister?' I'd never do that. It's dangerous. And he's always going down the Mucky Beck on his own. I never do that – I always go with the others.

'I never go down the Mucky Beck on my own, Mum. I'm not daft. I'm not like Norbert Lightowler.'

She'd leaned across the table and put her face really close to mine.

'You're not to go down there any more, do you understand?'

'Never?'

'Never!'

'Not even with the others?'

That's when she'd got her mad up.

'You don't go down there! Right? End of story!'

So that's why I don't go down the Mucky Beck any more. I'd like to but if my mum found out ... Well, my life wouldn't be worth living ...

The note was still going round the class. David Nunn was reading it. He nodded at Arthur and passed it on. What did it say? I was dying for it to come round to me. Geoff Gower had it now – he's only two desks away. He passed it to Normington who sits next to me and then just my luck, Bleasdale stopped marking.

'All right boys, stop writing. You should have finished by now. Who didn't complete that translation?'

Norbert put his hand up.

'What a surprise, Lightowler ...'

He looked at his watch.

'Right, we're going to spend the last ten minutes before the bell goes going over those first conjugation verbs ...'

He turned round and while he was rubbing the blackboard clean Norbert made a face at him.

'Not one of you got them all correct ...'

Norbert stopped – just in time.

' ... apart from McDougall.'

Bleasdale started writing on the board and we all jeered – quietly – and Norbert wrote 'SWOT' on a piece of paper and held it up. He always comes top in Latin does Alan McDougall.

'*Festino* – I hurry . . . *Ceno* – I dine . . . *Conor* – I try . . . Not hard enough some of you . . .'

While he had his back to us I held my hand out to Normington for Boocock's note and he gave it to me.

> *Meeting. Smokers corner. Dinner-time.*
> <u>*Don't tell the Pigeon.*</u> *Pass it on.*

'*Voco* – I call . . . *Celo* – I hide . . . *Postulo* – I demand . . . *Postulo* that you all learn these verbs at home tonight. There will be a test tomorrow . . .'

Everybody groaned. I looked at the note again. He'd underlined 'Don't tell the Pigeon'. That was the new lad. Why shouldn't we tell the new lad? What was Boocock going to do? He's a bully is Arthur Boocock. Everybody's scared of him. Except Gordon Barraclough. That's 'cos he's a bully too.

'*Pugno* – I fight . . .'

He'll hit you for anything will Arthur Boocock. He's got funny hair, tight little curls, and he hates it and once a lad from 3B called him 'Curly' and Boocock went mad. He smashed him. He was a lot bigger, this lad, and two years older but Arthur pulverised him. Another time when I was standing in the dinner queue talking to Keith Hopwood I'd tried on his glasses, just for fun and said everything looked a bit fuzzy. I'd had to shout 'cos it was noisy and Arthur Boocock had turned round and said 'Don't you call me fuzzy' and thumped me.

'*Oppugno* – I attack . . .'

He'd started on Monday, the new lad. I feel sorry for him. His mum had brought him on his first day. That's why I feel sorry for him. We have English first thing on a Monday with Melrose. I hate Mondays and I hate Melrose. We have Melrose for English then we have him for football straight after. When we went into the classroom he was standing talking to the new lad and his mum.

'Come along, boys, quick as you can, please, settle down . . .'

That's what I hate about Melrose. Any other time he'd be shouting and hitting us but whenever there's a parent there it's all 'Come along, boys, quick as you can, please, settle down.'

'We've got a new boy starting today. This is William Rothman. He's moved here from London. William, would you like to take that desk in the second row, next to Keith.'

If his mum hadn't been there it would have been 'Rothman, sit there, next to Hopwood.' Just as he'd been about to sit down, his mum had done something terrible. She'd kissed him – right in front of us all. Everybody'd started giggling, and trying to be quiet had made Norbert snort and that'd made us laugh even more. Melrose had looked at us and the vein under his eye had started to throb. That'd made us shut up. The new boy, his face all red, had sat down. I'd felt so sorry for him. If my mum ever kissed me in front of the class . . . well, I'd just want to die. I suppose that's how he felt. He hadn't looked at anybody, he'd just stared at his desk. I'd felt so sorry for him. And it had got worse. Just as she'd been about to go his mum had turned at the door.

41

'Sank you, boys, I'm sure Villiam vill be OK viz such nice boys as you . . .'

That's how she talks, sort of funny.

' . . . But you vill look after my little pigeon, von't you?'

Everybody'd tried their best not to laugh, even Melrose. The new lad had just kept looking down and as soon as his mum had gone we'd all burst out laughing. We couldn't help it.

'All right, all right, that's enough, calm down . . . You'll frighten the little pigeon.'

And that'd made us laugh even more. He's rotten is Melrose.

'*Voco* – I call . . . *Veto* – I forbid . . .'

I didn't nod at Boocock, I just passed the note to Keith Hopwood. He read it and I watched the Pigeon hold his hand out to take it. But of course Hopwood didn't give it him, he passed it to Douglas Hopkinson who sits in front of him in the front row. You could see the Pigeon wondering what was going on. I felt so sorry for him. Everybody called him the Pigeon now.

'*Ceno* – I dine . . . *Indico* – I judge . . .'

The bell went and we started putting our books away.

'Now think on, I want all those learning for tomorrow. I'm going to test you.'

Norbert started grumbling on the way out.

'It's not blooming fair. He shouldn't be giving us any homework. We have Geography and French on a Thursday, not Latin.'

'Are you complaining, Lightowler?'

'No sir . . .'

Smokers' Corner is at the top end of the playground in

42

the shelter under the woodwork classroom. It's where Boocock and Barraclough and all that lot go to smoke their cigarettes during break. I tried it once. It was horrible. It made me cough and I nearly threw up and they all laughed at me. And I got a sore throat. They all think they're so good, big men puffing away at their fags, blowing the smoke down their noses. They only do it to keep in with Boocock and his gang. I never go up to that end of the school yard, I just keep out of it. But I couldn't keep out of it now. I had to go. We all had to go. Boocock's orders. If you didn't you'd get thumped. I could see the others heading for the shelter. I wondered what it was all about. So did the Pigeon. He was watching them.

'Where are they all going?'

He didn't talk like us. He didn't talk funny like his mum, he talked sort of . . . well, sort of posh. If only he was a bit more like us maybe he wouldn't get teased so much.

'What's happening?'

I didn't know what to say to him.

'Y'what . . .?'

'Everybody seems to be going to the top end of the playground. Where are they all going?'

It would have to be me he was asking.

'Er . . .'

What was I supposed to say?

'Er . . .'

'That note you were all passing round. It was about me, wasn't it?'

'Er . . .'

'That's why they're all going up there, isn't it? It's something to do with me.'

43

'I don't know . . .'

It was true, I didn't know. Boocock's note had said
'Don't tell the Pigeon' but it didn't mean it was about him.
Maybe he just didn't want him there 'cos he's new . . . I
didn't know . . .

He wears these glasses with really thick lenses and black
frames and he took them off and cleaned them with his
hanky. He screwed up his eyes and looked towards the top
of the playground.

'*I* know . . .'

He put his glasses back on and wandered off. I called
after him.

'See you later, Pigeon – er, Rothman – William . . .'

He didn't turn round, he just carried on walking towards
the cloakrooms.

I heard Norbert calling me.

'C'mon – we're all waiting!'

I watched the Pigeon going in then ran up to Smokers'
Corner.

They were all puffing away at their cigarettes. Well, not
all of them, Boocock and Barraclough of course, Geoff
Gower, Kenny Spencer, Norbert, Holdsworth, Normington,
Duggie Bashforth, Douglas Hopkinson and most of the
others. Keith Hopwood looked sick. Alan McDougall wasn't
smoking, he was on guard. That's why they never got caught
– there was always somebody keeping watch. Boocock puffed
on his fag. He took a deep breath, held the smoke inside for
ages and then blew it out. He didn't cough. He never coughs.

'What were you talking to him about?'

Some spit shot out from the gap between his two top

teeth. They all do that when they're smoking. It just missed me.

'Nowt. He was just asking where everybody was going.'

'What did you say?'

'Nowt. He asked me if the note that was going round was about him.'

'What did you say?'

'Nowt.'

More spit. This time it was Barraclough and it didn't miss me, it just caught my shoe.

'Watch it, Barraclough.'

He just sneered at me and blew some smoke in my face while Boocock took another puff.

'Well I'll tell you all summat about the Pigeon . . . He's a Jerry!'

We all looked at him. Nobody knew what to say. Keith Hopwood took a drag on his cigarette and coughed and looked at Boocock. He went all red, not 'cos of the smoke, because he was embarrassed.

'It just w-w-went down the wr-wr-wrong w-way, Arthur. Sorry . . .'

Boocock didn't look at him. He just wet his fingers, put his cigarette out and dropped it into the top pocket of his blazer.

'A bloomin' Jerry. In our class.'

The others started putting theirs out. Norbert put his in his shoe.

'You mean a German, Arthur?'

''Course I mean a German. Don't you know what a Jerry is?'

Norbert grinned.

'Well my gran has a jerry under the bed in case she has to go in the night.'

Everybody laughed. I laughed even though I've got a jerry under my bed 'cos we've got an outside lav.

'I don't care about your soddin' granny, Lightowler. The new lad's a German. That's why his mum talks funny.'

Nobody said anything. We weren't sure what we were meant to say. Barraclough put his cigarette out.

'How do you know, Arthur?'

'My dad told me. She came into our shop. Ordered this German magazine.'

Arthur's mum and dad have got a newsagent's and tobacconist's just off Cranley Street. That's how he gets all his cigarettes. He nicks 'em.

'His dad talks funny an' all. They're all bloomin' Germans, whole family.'

I couldn't see what he was making such a fuss about. The Pigeon doesn't talk funny.

'Well, I don't think the new lad's a German. He talks just like us only a bit posher.'

Boocock screwed his face up and came towards me. I thought he was going to hit me for a minute.

''Course he's a bloody German. His mum and dad are German, that makes him a German and it's like my dad says, you fight the Nazis for six years and then they come and live next door to you. It's not right!'

They all started agreeing and mumbling to each other, saying it wasn't right, and Norbert crouched down and started moving about like a boxer.

'You mean he's a Nazzi? The Pigeon's a Nazzi?'

''Course he is. My dad says all Germans are Nazis, and

we shouldn't kid ourselves they're not. That's what my dad says.'

Boocock was talking rubbish. Not all Germans were Nazis, I don't care what his dad says. A lot of Germans ran away from the Nazis. I'd seen a picture at the Gaumont a couple of weeks back with my mum and my Auntie Doreen. It was all about this family escaping from Berlin. That's what it was called, *Escape from Berlin*. It was an 'A' film. It was great.

'I think you're wrong, Arthur. A lot of Germans ran away from the Nazis.'

Some of the others had seen *Escape from Berlin* and agreed with me. Norbert had seen it. He'd probably asked a stranger to take him in.

'He's right, Arthur. A lot of Germans had to escape from the Nazzies. You ought to go and see *Escape from Berlin*, it's great. It's an "A" though, you'll have to get someone to take you in.'

I don't know why Norbert calls them Nazzies when they're called Nazis. They weren't called Nazzies in *Escape from Berlin*. Boocock looked at us all and some more spit shot out from between his teeth.

'All right, the Pigeon might not be a Nazi but he's a German and we fought them in the war, didn't we? They're our enemy.'

What was Boocock talking about? The war's been over for nearly ten years. My mum says we've got to forgive and forget. He wouldn't be at our school if he was our enemy. His mum and dad wouldn't live in England, would they?

'And I'll tell you summat else . . .'

He stopped.

'Push off, Pigeon! This is private!'

We all turned round and saw him standing there, staring at us through his thick glasses. I wondered how long he'd been listening.

'Go on, push off, you little squirt! This is nowt to do with you.'

He didn't push off. He took a step closer. He went right up to Boocock.

'For your information, Boocock, my parents aren't German, they're from Austria. But I don't suppose you've heard of Austria, have you, Boocock? I could show it to you on a map if you like . . .'

We all stood there gawping. You don't talk to Arthur like that. Nobody talks to Arthur like that, not even Gordon Barraclough.

'And my father was in the British army as it happens. He fought against the Germans. And another thing, I was born in London. I'm English, Boocock, just like you.'

Boocock took a step in towards him. Oh no! If they have a fight Boocock'll pulverise him.

'You might be English, Pigeon, but you're not like me. You're not like any of us, are yer?'

We all looked at each other. What was he talking about? Norbert asked him.

'How do you mean he's not like any of us, Arthur? 'Cos he was born in London and talks different?'

Boocock looked at the Pigeon for a couple of seconds and sort of smiled. It was more of a sneer really.

'He knows what I mean . . .'

I didn't. What *did* he mean?

'It was his lot that killed Jesus . . .!'

48

What was he on about now? Who are 'his lot'?

'That's why he doesn't come to morning assembly. He's a Jew! And the Jews killed Jesus!'

We'd all wondered why every morning while we have assembly in the main hall, the Pigeon goes into a classroom at the back and always comes out after 'Our Father, who art in Heaven'. The first morning Reverend Dutton had taken him there David Holdsworth and me had heard him telling him when to come out.

'You sit in here, Rothman, and after the Lord's Prayer when you hear the Headmaster making the announcements, you can come out and join us . . .'

Boocock was still going on at him. I'd never seen a Jew before. He didn't look any different to me.

'That's why he brings his own dinner every day, in't it, Rothman? Our food's not good enough for you!'

The Pigeon's a lot smaller than Boocock and he was looking up at him through his thick glasses. He wasn't scared though. He didn't look it anyway. He just stood up to him, giving as good as he was getting.

'You're pathetic, Boocock.'

We were all waiting for Arthur to belt him one. But he didn't. I couldn't understand it. I don't think he was used to anybody standing up to him like that. He might have thumped him but he left it too late, the Pigeon just walked off. We all stood there, nobody knowing what to say . . . We could hear the bell going for dinner-time . . . Lads were starting to line up and I could hear Melrose telling them to stop talking . . . It was stupid, this, you couldn't blame the Pigeon for Jesus getting killed . . . It wasn't fair . . .

49

'Arthur, you can't blame the Pigeon for Jesus getting killed. It wasn't his fault, was it?'

The next thing Boocock had grabbed me by my shirt and had his face right close to mine. He nearly choked me.

'Listen you, you'd better make up your mind whose side you're on – the Jews or the Christians!'

He pushed me away and I grabbed this pillar to stop myself from falling. I grazed my hand and ended up on my bum with everybody looking down at me. They all followed Boocock to the dinner queue. Except Barraclough. He stood over me, a leg on either side.

'Yeah, you'd better make up your mind whose side you're on!'

And he kicked me.

From then on nobody spoke to the Pigeon. We all ignored him. Everybody. Me as well. He was always on his own. Every break. Every dinner-time. On the school bus to football. In the changing room. On the way to school. On the way home from school. Nobody talked to him. I knew it was wrong but I was a coward, I just did what all the others did. I was too scared of Boocock and Barraclough to do any different. I'd tried sticking up for him once and look what happened. It was all of us against him, the whole class. It must have been terrible for him. If it had been me I don't think I'd have gone to school. Or I'd have got my mum to talk to the headmaster or something. But the funny thing was, the Pigeon didn't seem that bothered. He didn't take any notice. He just carried on as if it wasn't happening. It was like *he* was ignoring *us*. And when anybody teased him he'd just smile. You'd have thought the teachers would have said something but they didn't seem to notice what was going

50

on. Melrose made it worse. One Friday the Pigeon brought in a letter for him.

'Ah, for me, Rothman – it's not often I get a letter by pigeon post.'

Everybody laughed. I laughed even though I didn't understand the joke, and the Pigeon just took off his glasses, wiped them on his hanky and gave one of his little smiles. Boocock sits in the front row and while Melrose was looking at the letter he turned round and whispered, loud enough for the Pigeon to hear.

'I bet it's from his mum asking us to be a bit nicer to her little pigeon . . .'

We all sniggered. The Pigeon just carried on wiping his glasses, he didn't seem to notice. Melrose finished reading the letter.

'So, Jewish festival is it on Monday? You won't be here? It's all right for some, eh Rothman?'

He put the letter in the envelope and gave it back to him.

'All right, lad, but you'd better give this to Mr Bleasdale, he's your form master.'

So it wasn't about us. I wish it had been. I'd have been glad if we'd all been told to stop it. Picking on him, ignoring him, treating him the way we were. Even if we'd got into trouble. Boocock couldn't do anything to us then, could he? Not if we'd been told by Melrose or the headmaster. I couldn't understand why the Pigeon didn't get his mum and dad to write. I would have.

Next morning I did my grocery round. I do it every Saturday. Ronnie Knapton used to do it and when his dad got a job in Leeds and they'd had to move I'd asked Mr Killerby if I could do it.

'How old are you, lad?'

'Eleven.'

Mr Killerby had sucked in his breath and shaken his head.

'I'm nearly twelve – I'm older than Ronnie Knapton!'

'Aye, but he's a big lad for his age. Can you ride a two-wheeler?'

What did he think I was, a little kid? Did he think I still rode round on a tricycle? I was one of the first in our street to ride a two-wheeler.

''Course I can, I've got a Raleigh three-speed.'

'Aye lad, but can you ride one of them with a full load?'

He'd pointed to the delivery bike standing in the back of the shop. It was a big black thing with old-fashioned handlebars and a basket at the front where the box of groceries went. The space between the crossbar and the pedals was closed in and on it was written KILLERBY'S – GROCERIES & PROVISIONS – FREE DELIVERY. If Ronnie Knapton could ride it I blooming well could. He wasn't that much bigger than me.

''Course I can.'

'Have you got your mum's permission?'

''Course I have.'

I hadn't. I'd thought I'd see if I got the job first.

'All right then lad, start Saturday. Half past nine. You should be finished by about half one. And you get three and six.'

Ronnie Knapton had got four shillings.

'Ronnie got four shillings . . .'

'Aye, but he started on three and six. We'll see how you get on.'

I'd asked my mum as soon as I'd got back from seeing Mr Killerby and of course she'd said no.

'Absolutely not, you're far too young!'

'I'm older than Ronnie Knapton.'

'You might be, but he's bigger than you.'

Blimey, you'd think Ronnie Knapton was a giant the way people go on. If it hadn't been for my Auntie Doreen she wouldn't have changed her mind. My Auntie Doreen thought it was a good idea.

'I think it's very commendable, Freda. Let him earn a bit of pocket money. It's not as if he's delivering papers, wandering round in the dark like a lot of them do. He'll be riding a bike. That's what he does on a Saturday morning anyway . . .'

I've been doing it for about six weeks now. Whenever I ask Mr Killerby how I'm getting on he says all right but he still only gives me three and six. Some of the people I deliver to give me money though. There's one old lady, Miss Boothroyd, she always gives me threepence, every week. Even if she's not there and I have to leave the box on the back step there's always an envelope that says *Killerby's Delivery Boy* with a threepenny piece inside. She's nice. At another house they always give me a glass of orange squash. The worst delivery is to a house at the top of Thornton Hill – it's so steep – but it's great on the way back.

That Saturday, after I'd got back from Thornton Hill, I parked the bike and went through to the back of the shop to get my next box. When a delivery's ready to take, Mr Killerby writes the name on a scrap of paper and puts it on top of the groceries, so I started sorting through my boxes. That's when I saw it – *Rothman, 12 Oak Park Crescent*. He only puts the address when it's a new customer. I was looking at it when Mr Killerby came in from serving in the shop.

'No lad, leave that till last. They're a Jewish family. They have their Sabbath on a Saturday, so they've gone to church. They said they'll be back after one.'

I did the rest of my deliveries, got my threepence from Miss Boothroyd, and at ten past one I was turning into Oak Park Crescent and looking for number twelve. I was hoping there'd be nobody in and I could leave the stuff on the back doorstep. I didn't want to see the Pigeon. I wouldn't have known what to say to him.

It was a big house with its own drive. It's quite a posh road, Oak Park Crescent. All the houses are big but a lot of them have been turned into flats. On the front gate there was a sign, DR JULIUS ROTHMAN, with lots of letters after his name. Underneath it gave the surgery hours. I didn't know the Pigeon's dad was a doctor. But then I didn't know anything the Pigeon. Nobody did. We never talked to him.

I pushed the bike up the drive past a sign that said SURGERY with an arrow underneath pointing to the back of the house. I went to the front door and rang the bell. Nothing. I rang again. Still nothing. There was nobody in. Thank goodness. I took the box of groceries round the back, left it on the step and just as I was getting on the bike they came walking up the drive. The Pigeon was talking to his dad and didn't see me at first. His mum smiled at me.

'Ah, are you bringing my sings from Mr Killerby, za grocer?'

I nodded.

'Yes, they're round the back. Mr Killerby told me to leave it there if you weren't in.'

'Zat's fine.'

She said something to the Pigeon's dad.

'Schatzi, gib den Kleinen ein paar Pennies.'

I couldn't understand what she was saying but his dad started searching in his pockets.

'Here you are, young man, a little somesing for your troubles.'

Boocock was right, his dad talked funny as well. He held out a shilling for me. A shilling!

'No, it's all right. Honestly.'

If it had been anybody else I'd have taken it like a shot but it wasn't right. We were all being horrible to the Pigeon at school and here was his dad wanting to give me a shilling. It wasn't right. But he kept on holding it out.

'I can't. P—'

I just stopped myself from calling him Pigeon.

'William, tell him.'

His mum looked at the Pigeon, then at me.

'You know each uzzer?'

The Pigeon smiled and told her my name.

'We go to the same school, mummy. We're in the same class.'

She asked me to come into the house and have something to eat with them.

'No, no thank you. I can't. I've got more deliveries to do . . .'

I couldn't stand it. They were being so nice to me. I just wanted to get away.

'I've got to go!'

I started to get on the bike but his mum came over and took hold of my hands.

'I vant to sank you. All of you. You have been so kind to my Villiam. He tells me every day vot good friends you are. It's not easy to join a new school and you have all made him feel so velcome . . .'

Then she smiled and squeezed my hands.

I felt sick. I wanted to throw up. I wanted to tell her the truth. We're horrible to your William. We don't talk to him 'cos Arthur Boocock says the Jews killed Jesus. 'Cos Arthur Boocock's a bully and we're all scared of him. 'Cos I'm a coward and I don't want them all not talking to me like they don't talk to him . . .

'I've got to go, Mrs Rothman.'

I started cycling away. I heard the Pigeon calling and running after me. I had to stop at the end of the drive 'cos of the road. He caught me up and pressed the shilling into my hand.

'Don't worry. I won't tell Boocock.'

We looked at each other for a minute and I hated him. How could he tell his mum how nice we all were, how friendly we all were, how welcome we all made him? I wanted him to tell her the truth.

'Why don't you tell her, Pigeon, why don't you tell her?'

He looked at me through his thick glasses.

'She worries about me.'

He went up the drive and when he got to the front door he smiled. It wasn't one of his little smiles. It was a sad smile. I watched him go in.

I got on the bike and pedalled off as fast as I could. I went up Heaton Hill and when I reached the top I stopped and threw the shilling into Lilycroft reservoir. I threw it as far as I could. Then I cycled back to Mr Killerby's. I couldn't stop crying all the way . . .

THE PIGEON

PART TWO

On the Sunday morning we went to church, my mum, me and my Auntie Doreen. We go every week. It's boring. Boring hymns, boring sermon. Standing up, sitting down, standing up, kneeling down, standing up, sitting down. I hate it. While I'm sitting, standing and kneeling I daydream. That's the only way I can get through. I think about all sorts of things. Nice things. Going to the pictures or the fair. School holidays. Anything to make the time go quick. Sometimes I think about my Sunday dinner. I can spend the whole time in church thinking about lovely roast beef or roast lamb or roast pork. I don't know what my mum or my Auntie Doreen would say if they knew that when the Vicar says 'Let us pray' and we all kneel on those cushion things and put our heads on our hands all I'm praying for is roast beef and Yorkshire pudding . . . with lovely crunchy potatoes, just the way my mum makes them.

But on that Sunday I didn't think about any of those things. All I could think about was the Pigeon. I couldn't stop thinking about him.

'Let us pray . . .'

Everybody knelt down and closed their eyes.

'Our Father, which art in heaven . . .'

I looked at my mum on one side and my Auntie Doreen on the other. They had their eyes closed.

'Hallowed be thy name . . .'

I closed my eyes. I didn't pray for roast beef and Yorkshire pudding this time, I prayed properly.

'Please God, make Arthur Boocock leave William alone. I know he's a Jew and the Jews killed Jesus, but it's not his fault. William had nothing to do with it . . .'

I didn't call him Pigeon – it didn't seem right, not when you're praying.

'Please make Boocock stop picking on him . . . Let him be like everybody else in our class even if he is a Jew.'

That's when I heard it, a little voice inside my head.

'You don't have to be like all the others. You don't have to ignore him . . .'

It was like God was talking back to me.

'Be his friend. Talk to him. There's nothing stopping you.'

No, there's nothing stopping me – except that I'm a coward. If only I wasn't such a coward.

'Please God, make me not be a coward so that I can be William's friend even if the others aren't . . .'

'Don't be such a big Jessie . . .!'

He sounded more like my mum now.

'Look at William. He goes home every night and tells his mum how friendly you all are and how welcome you've made him.'

I know, God, I know. You don't have to tell me.

'*You* wouldn't do that. You'd go home crying. And you'd stay off school, wouldn't you? You're soft, you are.'

I know, I know. I told you, I'm a coward. I am soft. I don't know how the Pigeon does it – sorry, William. He's a titch. Tons smaller than me but he's not scared of Boocock.

Look at the way he stood up to him the other day. What was it he said? 'You're pathetic, Boocock!' Yeah, that was it. 'You're pathetic, Boocock!' Just like that . . . And the way he'd looked at Arthur, stared at him, daring him to hit him. Boocock would have thumped me. He did thump me and all I'd said was you couldn't blame the Pigeon for Jesus getting killed. Why didn't he thump the Pigeon? Why did he just let him walk away . . .? 'Cos he can tell . . . He knows the Pigeon isn't scared of him. Not like me . . .

'Please God, make something happen to Arthur Boocock so that it all stops.'

I didn't mean anything bad like getting run over or getting ill or . . . well I wouldn't have minded – I hate Arthur Boocock – but if he got run over I wouldn't want it to happen 'cos I'd prayed for it. No, I just wanted someone to pick on him like he picks on everyone else. Let him be the one who gets bullied for a change, then he'd know what it's like.

'Please God, make Arthur Boocock get bullied. Let him have a taste of his own medicine for once – please . . .!'

I dreamt about the Pigeon that night. It was horrible. I was delivering a box of groceries on Mr Killerby's bike, pedalling as fast as I could. The whole class was chasing me and shouting and throwing stones. Arthur Boocock was leading them and I pedalled faster and faster. But it was like there was no chain on the bike. The pedals went round but I wasn't getting anywhere. I looked back and saw Boocock being run over by this big truck. Then Boocock's mum and dad were chasing me, and Melrose. And they were all shouting 'Traitor, traitor' and they came closer and closer. And I pedalled faster and faster. Suddenly I was at the top of a hill, I think it was Thornton Hill but it was twice as

61

steep, no, much more than that, ten times as steep, it was a sheer drop and I started going down faster and faster. Then I saw, it wasn't groceries in the cardboard box – it was the Pigeon! He was tiny, about a foot high, sitting in the box at the front of the bike and he was smiling at me. We were going to crash and I was trying to scream but no sound came out and the Pigeon just kept on smiling. We were up in the air now, the bike was gone and the cardboard box and we were falling to the ground and the Pigeon was still smiling. He wasn't scared, not like me. He wasn't scared 'cos he had wings on his feet. He could fly. He flew off smiling while I was falling . . . falling . . . falling . . . Then I woke up. It was horrible. I didn't know where I was. I stared at the ceiling and at the wallpaper for what seemed like ages. Then I heard my mum calling me to get up and I realised that it was my wallpaper I was staring at.

'Come on, move yourself, it's ten to eight. If I have to come up there there'll be trouble.'

'Gower . . .'
    'Yes, sir.'
    'Hopkinson . . .'
    'Sir.'
    'Hopwood . . .'
    'Yes, sir.'
Monday morning. English with Melrose. Then football, with Melrose. I hate Mondays.
    'Illingworth . . .'
    'Yes, sir.'
    'Lightowler . . .'
    'Sir.'

'Stop slouching, Lightowler.'

'Yes, sir.'

I couldn't get the dream out of my head. It'd been so real. Boocock getting run over by that truck. It was like it had really happened. I looked over to his desk. I never thought I'd ever be pleased to see Arthur Boocock but I was today. He was messing about with a small mirror. Pollywashing. That's getting the sun in the mirror and shining it into someone's face. He was pollywashing Keith Hopwood, right in his eyes. Boocock kept shining the sun in his face, taunting him, and Hopwood was getting mad. He'd done the same thing to the Pigeon last week during history. He'd shone the sun into his eyes all during the lesson. But the Pigeon wasn't like Hopwood. He didn't go mad. He didn't do anything. He just carried on working as if it wasn't happening even though his left eye was watering like anything. He just didn't seem to notice.

'Rothman . . . Rothman.'

Melrose looked up and Boocock hid the mirror under his desk just in time.

'Rothman . . .?'

A few of them sang-song it together:

'Not here, sir.'

Melrose nodded and wrote in the register.

'Oh, that's right, Jewish holiday or some such nonsense. All right for some, eh lads?

'Yes, sir.'

'Spencer . . .'

'Sir.'

'Tattersall . . .'

'Yes, sir.'

All during English, whenever Melrose wasn't looking, Boocock carried on pollywashing Hopwood, making his eyes water even more. When the sun went behind a cloud he stopped and started flicking paper pellets instead. One got him right inside his ear. Later on, in the cloakroom, while we were getting our stuff for football Hopwood was grumbling and showing me his sore ear.

'I'll be glad when the P-Pigeon gets back and B-B-Boocock can start p-p-picking on him again.'

And I thought to myself, not just Boocock, we'll all be picking on him. You, me, everybody. 'Cos we're all scared of Boocock.

We don't have any playing fields at our school. We go on a special bus to Bankfield top, about two miles away. The bus was late and Melrose told us to wait inside the school gates.

'McDougall, fetch me when the bus comes. I'll be in the staff room. And *be quiet*! No messing about.'

Norbert made a face at Melrose behind his back.

'S'all right for him. We wait here and he goes off and has a nice cup of tea.'

Boocock was leaning against the wall, a stupid sneer on his face.

'Good. Gives me chance to have a fag.'

And he took a cigarette out of his top pocket. While he lit up the others looked around, nervous, in case anybody was at the classroom windows. Boocock wasn't bothered. Nothing ever scares him. Big 'ead! I watched him, leaning against the wall, showing off, holding his cigarette between his thumb and his big finger with the lit end tucked inside his hand so nobody could see it. And blowing smoke down

64

his nose. He thinks he's so good, doesn't he? He thinks he's so tough. He is . . . Why doesn't he ever cough? I wish the smoke would catch in his throat and make him cough. I wish he'd choke. Norbert was up on the school gates looking out for the bus.

'Bloomin' hummer – look at the Pigeon!'

We all looked through the gates. He was coming down the road with his mum and dad and they were all dressed up. They must have been on their way to their Jewish church.

His mum was wearing a big hat with cherries on it and round her shoulders she had this fur thing and it had an animal's head at one end. It looked like a fox's head. And his dad was wearing a bowler hat and the Pigeon was wearing a hat too. It wasn't a bowler but it was the sort of hat grown-ups wear. He looked stupid. They got nearer and everybody started whistling and shouting. His mum waved at us.

'Look, Villiam, all your nice schoolfriends are vaving to you.'

The Pigeon was blushing like anything. He sort of nodded and walked on, trying to get his mum and dad past as quick as he could, but she came over to us. Oh no, I didn't want her to see me. I didn't want her saying hello to me in front of all the others. I worked my way to the back and hid behind Duggie Bashforth and David Nunn.

'Hello, boys. I vant to say sank you to you all . . .'

I knew what she was going to say. I peeped at the Pigeon. He was cringing. He knew what she was going to say as well.

'You have made Villiam feel so velcome in his new school. He tells me every day vot good friends you are. His farzer and I really appreciate your kindness . . .'

65

She smiled. Nobody said anything. They all looked at each other. Someone laughed, I think it was Norbert, and that set some of the others off. The bus came and McDougall went off to fetch Melrose. I kept myself hidden behind Bashforth, crouching down a bit, making sure the Pigeon's mum couldn't see me.

'Vell boys, ve must go. Have a good game of football. Come along, Villiam.'

She said something to the Pigeon's dad in German or whatever language they talk and walked off. The Pigeon didn't follow, he stood there looking at us all. Then I realised, it wasn't the others he was looking at – it was me. He knew why I'd been hiding behind Duggie Bashforth and he was looking right at me like . . . well, like I was a piece of muck. All right, Pigeon, I'm not like you, I'm a coward, I don't want your mum to see me. She might say hello and the others would know I've been talking to you. You know what would happen then, don't you? Nobody would talk to *me*. I want to be friends with you but I daren't . . . Stop looking at me like that . . . Bloody bus. If it hadn't been late none of this would have happened . . . Stop looking at me, it's not my fault.

'Villiam, come now, ve are late . . .'

Go on, go, your mum's calling you. It's not my fault you're a Jew! He stayed looking at me a bit longer, then he shook his head and followed his mum and dad.

The others all burst out laughing and Barraclough started taking off his mum.

'Sank you for looking after my Villiam. You have made him feel so velcome in his new school . . .!'

They all laughed and Norbert and a few others took her off as well.

'Come on, Villiam, ve are late . . .'

'Vell boys, have a good game of football . . .'

'I vant to say sank you, you have made Villiam feel so velcome . . .'

'*Shut up!*'

I couldn't help it. It was like it was someone else shouting, not me.

'*Shut up!*'

They were all looking at me. My stomach was churning. Why had I shouted like that? Why hadn't I kept quiet? Boocock was looking at me. He came over. He put his face close to mine.

'Who are you telling to shut up?'

I could smell the cigarette on his breath. I wish someone had seen him smoking. I wish he'd got taken to the headmaster. I wish he'd got the cane. I wish he'd get expelled. I wish he'd leave me alone. It's not fair. Oh God!

'Well, it's not fair, Arthur, she can't help talking like that, she's not English.'

'That's right . . .'

He starting punching me in the chest, pushing me backwards.

' . . . and I've told you before, you want to make up your mind whose side you're on, the Jews or the Christians.'

He got hold of my shirt and twisted his hand round, choking me. I could hear Barraclough and a few others laughing.

'Come on, whose side are you on, theirs or mine?'

It's stupid, this, Boocock. The Pigeon's all right. His mum and dad are all right. Why do we have to choose sides? Why are you such a bully? I wish you'd die, Boocock.

'Yours, Arthur . . .'

He let me go. I don't know if it was 'cos I'd said I was on his side or 'cos he'd seen Melrose coming.

'Right, on the bus – and keep the talking down! Lightowler, what've you got in your mouth?'

'Chewing gum, sir.'

'Get rid of it.'

He spat it out.

'Not there, lad – in the bin!'

Nobody sat next to me on the bus. We were on the top deck while Melrose sat downstairs reading his paper like he always does. They were all talking and laughing and taking off the Pigeon's mum again. Well, let them. I wasn't going to say anything this time. It was nothing to do with me. Why should I worry about the Pigeon?

'W-w-what I c-can't understand is w-w-why he told h-his mum w-w-we're all his f-f-friends?'

'Cos he's not soft like you, Keith Hopwood, or me, or any of you. He doesn't want his mum to worry so he hasn't told her that we don't talk to him 'cos the Jews killed Jesus. And he's not scared of Boocock neither. I'd love to have said it, but I didn't dare. I didn't want to end up like him with no friends, with nobody talking to me.

Nobody did talk to me for the next sixty minutes. They shouted at me. I was in goal. We lost.

On the way back though everything was all right. It all seemed forgotten. Boocock and Barraclough were busy teasing Hopwood. They'd pinched one of his football boots and were hanging it out of the window pretending to drop it. I sat at the back with Norbert and David Holdsworth

68

playing I-Spy. Hopwood was going mad, he looked like he was going to cry.

'G-g-give it b-back, give it b-back or I'll tell. I'll r-report you . . .'

The more he shouted the more Boocock teased him. I heard Melrose coming up the stairs.

'Hey, Arthur – Melrose!'

He pulled the boot back through the window, gave it back to Keith and turned to the front. Melrose looked around for a few seconds, told us all to keep the noise down and went back downstairs. After he'd gone Boocock turned round and gave me the thumbs-up.

'Ta.'

I gave him the thumbs-up back and smiled.

'That's all right, Arthur.'

Yeah, everything was all right now. I was on Arthur's side and the Pigeon could look after himself. I wasn't going to stick up for him any more. I was going to keep my mouth shut. And I would have done if I hadn't met those Galsworthy Road lads on my way home from school.

Monday afternoons aren't so bad. Double woodwork, boring 'cos I'm no good at it, history which is my best subject – I got 48% in the test – and the last lesson is RI with Reverend Dutton. That's boring as well and we all mess about but he never seems to notice and we make fun of him 'cos he wears a wig. Even when he does get mad with any of us he always says sorry afterwards. He's not like a proper teacher, Reverend Dutton, he's too nice. When the bell goes everybody makes a mad rush for the cloakrooms even if he's in the middle of a sentence. You wouldn't dare do that with Melrose or Bleasdale or any of them.

'And so, boys, we read in St Luke 20 "that Jesus went into the Temple and began to cast out them that sold therein, and them that bought, saying unto them . . ." '

The bell went and we could hear Reverend Dutton still talking to us while we were running down the corridor.

'Thank you, boys, we'll pick up from there next time . . .'

I felt a smack on the back of my head.

'Where's the fire?'

It was Melrose.

'Nowhere, sir.'

'Then walk!'

He gave me another crack on the head and I walked the rest of the way. I could hear Hopwood shouting in the cloakroom.

'G-give it b-back, it's not f-fair, give it b-back.'

Boocock had pinched one of his boots again and him, Barraclough and Norbert were throwing it to each other.

'Come on L-Lightowler, g-give it 'ere.'

He tried to grab it but Norbert threw the boot to me. Oh, what was I supposed to do with it?

'Go on, g-give it to us. B-be a sp-sp-sport.'

I felt sorry for Hopwood but if I gave it to him they'd all have a go at me, wouldn't they? Same as sticking up for the Pigeon. All that happens is that *I* get picked on.

'Catch, Arthur!'

I lobbed it over his head. Stupid Hopwood tried to get it, fell over and caught his chin on one of the pegs.

'Aahh, bloody 'ell! Aahh!!'

He really hurt himself. He was rolling about on the floor screaming.

70

'My chin! My bloody chin! I'm gonna report you.'

The funny thing was he wasn't stammering. It was the first time I'd heard him talk without stammering.

'Aw my chin!'

'What's all the shouting about?'

Melrose! We looked at Hopwood. He was sitting on the floor still rubbing his chin.

'What are you doing down there, Hopwood? What's going on?'

'I f-f-fell, sir. I c-caught my ch-ch-chin o-o-on one of the pegs, sir . . .'

He looked at Boocock.

'It w-w-was an accident, sir.'

'Well get up and get off home. You shouldn't be mucking about in here. Come on, all of you, out!'

He went marching up the corridor shouting that if any of us were still there when he came back in three minutes we'd be there till six o'clock! Boocock kicked the football boot over to Keith.

'We was only havin' a bit of fun. You can't take a joke, you.'

Barraclough started taking him off.

'Yeah, we w-w-was only havin' a bit of f-f-fun.'

They went, laughing their heads off. I picked it up for him.

'Here you are, Keith.'

'S-s-sod off!'

My boots were tied together hanging on my peg, so I put them over my shoulder, got my bag and I went.

He asks for it, does Keith, screaming and shouting like that. He shouldn't take any notice of Boocock. He should just ignore him, he'd soon stop. Who am I to talk, mind? Why do I open my big mouth? So Arthur Boocock can thump me? Well not any more. I'll just go along with all the others. Keep out of trouble. Yes, once I'd made up my mind that I was on Boocock's side, that I was going to keep quiet, I felt much better. The Pigeon can fight his own battles, I'm gonna keep my mouth shut from now on.

I turned up St Paul's Terrace and that's when I saw them. These two lads sitting on a wall at the top of the road. They must have been about twelve or thirteen. They were bigger than me anyway. At first I thought they were feeding pigeons but when I got nearer I could see it wasn't bread they were throwing, it was gravel. They were looking at me so I crossed over.

'Grammar School ponce!'

I didn't look up. St Paul's Terrace goes into my road so I just kept walking. I wanted to get home as fast as I could.

'Yeah, Grammar School tart!'

Oh no, I bet they go to Galsworthy Road Secondary Modern. Please don't let them be Galsworthy Road lads.

'Not good enough for you, are we? Just 'cos we go to Galsworthy Road . . .'

Oh heck. They carry knives, Norbert had told me. And they hate Grammar School lads. I shouldn't have worn my blazer. I should have put it in my bag. I started walking a bit quicker. Not too quick, I didn't want them to see that I was scared. Oh no, they're crossing over. They're following me!

'You think you're good, don't yer, just 'cos you go to the Grammar School?'

They were behind me. I kept walking. I turned into my road. I could hear them following.

'Well you're not. We can lick you at anything. I could take you on one arm behind my back.'

The other one laughed.

'I could take him on both arms behind my back.'

It's a long road, ours, and we live right at the other end. All I had to do was reach home, then I'd run in and I'd be all right. I felt my trouser pocket to make sure I'd got my keys. Yeah, they were there. All I had to do was keep walking for a few minutes and I'd be all right.

'You're all soft, you Grammar School lot, you're all jessies.'

One of them kicked my heel and tried to trip me up. I didn't look round. I kept going. I just wanted to get home.

'Look, he daren't even look at us. He's soft.'

They caught me up and started shouldering me, one on each side, pushing me from one to the other. Why were they picking on me? 'Cos I'm at Grammar School? It's stupid. Same as picking on the Pigeon 'cos he's a Jew or picking on Reverend Dutton 'cos he wears a wig or Keith Hopwood 'cos he's got a stammer. It's stupid.

'Look at him, he's gonna cry. He's a big cry-baby . . .!'

'Yeah, big Grammar School cry-baby's gonna cry!'

They were right. I could feel the tears in my eyes. I was trying to stop myself but I couldn't. I was going to cry. Don't let me cry, please don't let me cry . . . Then I saw her. My mum! I couldn't believe it. She must have got off work early. She'd just turned into the road. I waved.

'Mum!'

She waved back. I was going to be all right.

'That's my mum. You'd better go if you don't want to get into trouble.'

73

They laughed. They weren't bothered.

'You think we're scared of your big fat mum?'

They waved – and she waved back at them and went inside. She went into the house. She left me with them.

'*Mum*!!'

They didn't thump me that hard. Just once in the stomach and they threw my bag and my boots over a wall into one of the gardens. Then they ran off.

'What are you crying for, love? What's happened?'

She sat me down in the kitchen and I told her all about it. I couldn't stop crying.

'Why did you go in? Why didn't you wait?'

It was stupid saying that, it wasn't her fault.

'I didn't know, love. I thought they were your friends.'

She was sitting next to me, her arm round my shoulder. The tears were running down my cheeks. But I wasn't crying about what had just happened. It was everything else. Everything that had been happening with the Pigeon. It wasn't right. I knew it wasn't right and I decided. I wasn't going to be on Boocock's side.

I got to school early next morning and looked for him. He was bottom end of the playground on his own as usual. He was sitting on his bag, reading. My heart was thumping.

'Hi, William.'

He looked up, surprised.

'Hello.'

I fished out the bag of sweets I'd bought.

'Do you want a Nuttall's Mintoe?'

'Thank you . . .'

He was just going to take one but stopped. I could see

him looking behind me. I turned round. Boocock, Barraclough, Norbert and Hopwood and a few others were coming towards us. My heart started thumping even more. He didn't say anything. He just stood staring at me.

'I'm not gonna be on your side, Arthur. I think it's stupid. I don't think we should have sides.'

I was still holding the bag of sweets. Boocock looked at me.

'Traitor!'

He would have hit me but William stepped in front and thumped him right in the stomach – hard. Boocock couldn't believe it. None of us could. He couldn't speak. I think it was 'cos he was winded but it might have been 'cos he was surprised, I wasn't sure. He got his mad up then and went for William – and William hit him again. Harder. I looked at Boocock lying on the ground, holding his stomach and crying. God had answered my prayers at last. Boocock was getting a taste of his own medicine. And all I could think was that it was a good job I *hadn't* prayed for anything bad to happen to him, like getting run over or getting ill.

William went back and sat on his bag and started reading again. I followed him.

'You're a good fighter, William.'

He looked up and smiled.

'My father says we must only use violence as a last resort. I think that was a last resort, don't you?'

I didn't know what he was talking about. I held out the bag of sweets.

'Here, have a Nuttall's Mintoe . . .'

75

THE PIGEON

PART THREE

William doesn't go to our school any more. He goes to a boarding school where there's more Jews. I think his mum and dad thought it was better for him. I still see him in the holidays and I see his mum and dad every Saturday when I take their groceries. His dad always gives me a shilling. It's a shame he went to another school 'cos by the time he left everybody liked him – except Boocock.

THE YO-YO CHAMPION

'Black suede crêpe-soles! For school? Do you hear that, Doreen?'

My Auntie Doreen hadn't heard 'cos she was reading my mum's *Woman's Weekly*. We'd just had our tea. Gammon and chips and a pineapple ring, my favourite. My Auntie Doreen always comes for tea on a Friday and she always brings the gammon. She works on the bacon counter at the Co-op. I think she gets it for free.

'What was that, Freda?'

My mum poured herself another cup of tea.

'We're going to Crabtree's tomorrow morning to get his Lordship some new school shoes and do you know what he wants? Black suede crêpe-soles. Like those teddy boys wear. Black suede crêpe! For school!'

They both laughed and my mum shook her head as if suede crêpe shoes were the daftest thing in the world. It wasn't fair. Arthur Boocock's mum and dad had let him get some, and Kenny Spencer's. So had Gordon Barraclough's. Tony had got some as well. And David Holdsworth. Even Keith Hopwood said he was getting some – but I don't believe him. He's soft, is Keith Hopwood. He was just saying it to keep up with all the others.

'But Mum, everybody's getting them. Tony's got a pair.

Even Keith Hopwood's getting some. Keith Hopwood! Everybody's getting them.'

'Well you're not. You'll have proper black leather lace-ups. Proper school shoes and I don't want you playing football in them neither.'

My Auntie Doreen didn't help. She said that black suede shoes were very vulgar and my mum gave her a funny sort of look and smiled.

'I know why *you* don't like black suede shoes . . .'

My Auntie Doreen gave her a funny look back.

'Yes, and he was very vulgar too, just like his shoes . . .'

And she smiled as well. They're always doing that, my mum and my Auntie Doreen, saying things to each other that I can't understand and then smiling their secret smiles.

'Who's vulgar just like his shoes?'

I don't know why I bothered asking. I knew they wouldn't tell me. They never tell me.

'Oh, just someone your Auntie Doreen knew a long time ago.'

Then they did it again. Smiled at each other. Did they think I didn't notice? Well I did notice. I always notice. But I can never understand what they're smiling about.

I didn't care. All I cared about was getting some black suede crêpes. Who said school shoes have to be black leather lace-ups anyway? It wasn't fair.

'Who says school shoes have to be black leather lace-ups anyway? What's wrong with black suede crêpes? Who says you can't wear black suede crêpes?'

As soon as I said it I knew I shouldn't have. My mum banged her fist on the table. She made me jump. She made my Auntie Doreen jump. And she spilt her tea.

'I do! I say you can't wear black suede crêpes. Now fetch me a cloth.'

I didn't say anything more about my new shoes 'cos the big red blotch had come up on her neck. She always gets it when she's upset or excited and I know that's when to shut up. I fetched the cloth from the kitchen and gave it to her.

'I'm sorry, Mum . . .'

She didn't say anything, she just mopped up where she'd spilt the tea. But the blotch was starting to fade. Thank goodness . . .

Crabtree's is the big posh department store in town and we always go there to buy my new school shoes. It takes ages. You have to take a ticket with a number on, then sit down and wait for your number to be called out. We took our ticket and sat down.

'Sixty . . . Ticket number sixty . . .?'

I liked coming to Crabtree's. Not with my mum, that's boring, but I sometimes go after school with Norbert and Tony and anybody else who wants to. The first time we went was to look at the 'moving staircases'. Norbert told me about them. I didn't believe him.

'Moving staircases! How can a staircase move?'

I laughed and Norbert got quite cross.

'I'm telling you, I was in Crabtree's on Saturday and they've got moving staircases now. I went on them.'

I was sure he was having me on. I'd been in Crabtree's lots of times. I'd been up and down in the lifts but I'd never seen a moving staircase.

'Well, how do they work then, these moving staircases?'

'You stand on the first step and you go to the top and then you get off.'

'How do you go down?'

Norbert looked at me as if I was stupid.

'They've got moving staircases that go down as well.'

I couldn't see it. I just couldn't imagine a staircase that moved. It was impossible.

'It's impossible. How can a staircase move?'

'We'll go down to Crabtree's after school and you can see for yourself.'

And we did. And Norbert was right, they did have moving staircases. I couldn't believe it. We went from the ground floor up to the fifth floor and then down again. We did it three times. Then we got thrown out 'cos Norbert started walking down one of the moving staircases that was going up.

We often go to Crabtree's after school. We go up and down in the lifts or on the moving staircases and look at all the toys and at Christmas they have a grotto and you can walk through for free. And sometimes they have a stand and give things away. One time there was a lady asking people to try bits of cheese. Norbert and me went back three times before she realised and told us to push off. I didn't like it – it tasted of soap – but it was free. Another time they were asking people to try Ribena and gave away miniature bottles. We got two each. The one thing I don't like about going with Norbert is that he pinches things. I don't know how he does it. They never see him. *I* never see him and I'm with him all the time. I don't even know *why* he does it. He steals things he doesn't even want. He throws them away. One time it was a reel of blue cotton. Another time it was a wooden spoon. The last time we'd come out of Crabtree's it was a ball of wool he'd taken.

'Why do you do it, Norbert? You're going to get caught one day.'

He grinned at me.

'That's why I do it – to see if they can catch me . . .'

Then he laughed and threw the ball of wool in a rubbish bin. He's mad. He just likes stealing. Mind you, his dad's in prison for thieving. Maybe it runs in the family.

'Sixty-one . . . Ticket sixty-one . . .?'

My mum was in quite a good mood so I'd decided I was going to give it one last go, see if I could persuade her to get me black suede crêpes. It was just a matter of choosing the right moment.

'Sixty-one . . . Number sixty-one . . .?'

A fat man with a red face and a long droopy moustache held up his hand.

'Sixty-one? Over 'ere, and about bloody time . . .'

My mum looked at him and tutted to herself. She doesn't like swearing.

'Twenty minutes I've been waiting. Over twenty bloody minutes. Bloody ridiculous!'

My mum wriggled in her chair and tutted again while this lady apologised to the fat man.

'I'm very sorry, sir, but Saturdays are our busy day. We're serving as fast as we can.'

'Aye, well you need more bloody staff then, don't you? Over twenty minutes to get from ticket bloody fifty-eight to sixty-bloody-one? Bloody ridiculous!'

That's when my mum got her mad up.

'Do you mind not using that kind of language? There's children present.'

My mum wriggled in her chair again and folded her arms. Everybody was looking at us and I could feel myself going red. Why did she have to interfere like that? It was none of our business. That's what the fat man thought as well.

'You mind your own bloody business, it's nowt to do with you . . .' and he mumbled something about 'bloody busy-bodies'.

'It is my business if you swear in front of my young lad. I'll thank you to keep your foul language to yourself.'

The fat man suddenly stood up. He came over and glared at my mum.

'I'm not shopping 'ere. I'll take my bloody money elsewhere . . .!'

And he stormed out. It all went quiet. My mum was shaking a bit and I could see the red blotch on her neck. That was it. I could forget about my suede crêpes now.

'Sixty-two . . . Ticket sixty-two . . .?'

The lady who'd been serving the fat man came over to us.

'I'm sorry about that, madam.'

My mum was still sitting up straight with her arms folded.

'There's no need for that kind of language. Not in Crabtree's anyway.'

The lady had a badge on her jacket that said Assistant Manager.

'Especially not in Crabtree's, madam. We've had trouble with him before. I think he's a bit funny.'

84

'Ticket sixty-three . . . Sixty-three . . .?'

The assistant manager apologised again and went off to serve number sixty-three. It was a woman with a ginger-headed lad that I sort of knew. I've seen him around. He goes to St Bede's. I don't like him. I see him sometimes on my way home from school when I cut through the park. He and his mates are always hanging round the swings. They smoke. And they have spitting competitions. They go as high as they can on the swings and see who can spit the furthest. It's disgusting. He was staring at me so I stared back . . . Once on my way home from school I'd thought he was going to hit me. A few of them were sitting on the roundabout going round slowly. He'd jumped off and stood in front of me. I'd been scared stiff. He'd put his face right close to mine.

'Who are you for, Churchill or Attlee?'

I hadn't known what he was on about.

'Come on, who are you for, Churchill or Attlee?'

I didn't know what to say. I wasn't for either of them. He'd put his face even closer, our noses were nearly touching.

'I'm only asking you once more, kid. Churchill or Attlee, who are you for?'

'Churchill . . .'

He'd smiled.

'That's all right, then.'

And he'd gone back to the roundabout. I dread to think what would have happened if I'd said Attlee. I'd only said Churchill 'cos I knew he was the Prime Minister . . . While his mum was talking to the assistant manager Copper-nob and me carried on staring at each other . . . He won – I looked away. When I looked back he was still staring at me and he put his tongue out at me. I looked away again.

'What's our number, mum?'

She showed me. Seventy-two.

'Seventy-two? It's going to take ages!'

She turned on me and put her face close to mine, like the ginger-headed lad did in the park that day.

'Don't you start. I've had enough with that nasty man!'

Copper-nob was staring at me again, sneering, watching me getting told off by my mum.

'Sixty-four . . . Ticket number sixty-four . . .'

The fat man was right. It was taking ages . . . Oh no, Copper-nob was trying on black suede crêpes! It wasn't fair.

'Mum . . .'

'Mm . . .?'

'I was just wondering . . .'

'What?'

'I was just wondering . . .'

The red blotch was still there.

' . . . if I could go and look at the toys? It's going to be a while before they get to seventy-two.'

She looked at her watch.

'Ten minutes. Back here by twenty past. No later.'

'Thanks, Mum.'

I ran out. Copper-nob was walking up and down trying on his new shoes and I could hear the assistant manager telling his mum how good suede crêpes were.

'They're very durable, madam. Last for ever. All the lads are wearing them.'

Yeah, all the lads except me.

I love the toy department in Crabtree's, there's so much

to look at. They've got the biggest display of lead soldiers anywhere. (That was another thing that Norbert pinched once, two lead soldiers and a cannon – he didn't throw them away.) On the ceiling there's all these wire tracks and hanging from them are little carriages. When you buy something the assistant puts your money into one of the carriages, pulls a handle and the carriage zooms across the ceiling to another assistant sitting in a cash desk behind a glass screen and she sends the carriage back with the change. It's fantastic watching all these carriages zooming all over the place.

Sometimes they have people doing special toy demonstrations. Like the spinning top that you could balance on the point of a pencil or the rim of a glass and it spun for ages. It cost half-a-crown, a special demonstration price. Once a lady was showing how you could make your own balloons. She squeezed this coloured stuff out of a tube, rolled it into a ball, stuck in a plastic straw and blew it into a balloon. That was half-a-crown as well. Everything they demonstrate always seems to cost half-a-crown.

'Just two and sixpence. A half-a-crown for the Lumar yo-yo . . .'

That's when I saw him. Well, I heard him first. I was looking at the lead soldiers, they'd had some new ones in. Irish guards. I turned round.

'The best yo-yo money can buy for only two shillings and sixpence. The price of a fish and chip supper . . .'

There he was, a yo-yo in each hand, doing these wonderful tricks.

'The Lumar yo-yo will last a lifetime . . .'

On his stand was a big poster, *Don Martell – Yo-yo Champion of Great Britain*, and there was a photo. It showed him doing his yo-yo tricks. He looked a lot younger and he was wearing a bow tie. A few people were watching and I went over.

'Come closer, don't be shy. I'm going to show you how the yo-yo can give you hours of pleasure. After just a few minutes' practice you too will be "walking the dog" . . .'

And he sent the yo-yo spinning down to the floor. When it reached the end of the string it spun round and round and then he walked towards us and the yo-yo rolled along the ground, just like a dog on a lead. He flicked his wrist and the yo-yo went flying up in the air. Another flick and it disappeared into his hand.

'Walking the dog, ladies and gentlemen, a yo-yo trick any one of you here today can master within minutes. You!'

He was pointing at me.

'Me?'

'Yes you, young man. Do I know you?'

Everybody turned round and looked.

'No.'

'We have never met?'

'No.'

'Please step forward.'

I felt myself going all red as I went towards him.

'Now, young man, which hand do you write with?'

I held out my right hand.

'This one.'

The Yo-yo Champion picked up a red yo-yo and fixed the string on my big finger.

'Just do what I do.'

He flicked the yo-yo out of the back of his hand towards the floor and it stayed spinning round at the end of the string like before. There was no way that I was going to do that. But I flicked it out of my hand just like he showed me and I couldn't believe it. It was spinning just like his.

'I don't believe it, ladies and gentlemen, look at that.'

There was my yo-yo at the end of the string spinning round and round. It looked like it could have gone on for ever.

'Let's see if he can "walk the dog".'

He turned sideways, let his yo-yo drop to the floor and started walking. With my yo-yo still spinning I copied him. I let it slowly drop down to the floor. It worked. The yo-yo rolled along the ground and I followed it. I was walking the dog just like Don Martell.

Everybody was clapping as he flicked his yo-yo up in the air and then flicked it back into his hand. He turned to watch me. I flicked my hand just like he'd done and the yo-yo flew up into the air. Another flick and it rolled up the string and I caught it in my hand.

'The lad's a natural. A future champion, which is very important because next Saturday, a week today, we will be holding a competition here in the store to find the Yo-yo Champion. First prize will be a grand silver cup inscribed with the champion's name and a Crabtree's gift token to the value of ten pounds.'

A silver cup and a ten pound token. I could go in for it . . . if I had a yo-yo.

'And I am selling the world-famous Lumar yo-yo at the special demonstration price of a half-a-crown. Two shillings and sixpence.'

Half a crown . . . Maybe my mum would get me one . . . My mum! I looked at the clock which was above the lady who took the money in the cash desk. Half past! She'd told me to be back by twenty past. Oh no! I started to run off.

'Oi! I'm not giving them away, young man. Half-a-crown.'

I still had the yo-yo in my hand. I'd forgotten. I ran back, took the string off my finger and gave it to him.

'Sorry – I'm late for my mum.'

I didn't know which would be quicker, the lift or the moving staircase. I looked up at the lights that tell you which floor the lift is on. The 'G' was lit up. It was on the ground floor. The lift would be quicker. Come on, lift, come on . . . The 'G' went out and a couple of seconds later the doors opened.

'Basement-*ah*. Toys-*ah*, Household Goods-*ah*, Electrical Goods-*ah* . . .'

He always talked like that, the man who worked the lift. It makes me and Norbert laugh.

'Basement-*ah*. Toys-*ah*, Household Goods-*ah*, Electrical Goods-*ah* . . .'

He only had one arm. His other arm was just an empty sleeve pinned across his chest. I went in the lift and who do you think was coming out in his brand new black suede crêpes? Lucky beggar. He looked at me and gave me one of his sneery lop-sided grins.

'Mind the doors-*ah*.'

We started going up. Shoes were on the second floor.

'Ground Floor-*ah*. Haberdashery-*ah*, Furnishing Fabrics-*ah*, Glassware-*ah* . . .'

Come on, come on! If we missed our turn my mum was going to go mad. We started moving again, thank goodness.

90

'First Floor-*ah*. Ladies' Fashions-*ah*, Knitwear-*ah*, Cafeteria . . .'

I suppose it was impossible to say 'Cafeteria-*ah*'. Come on! Why couldn't they all hurry up? I could see people going up the moving staircase. I ran out and started running up the moving stairs – it had to be quicker. It would have been if it hadn't been for these two women. They wouldn't let me go past.

I asked nicely.

'Excuse me.'

They just ignored me.

'Excuse me.'

One of them looked at me then turned away and they carried on talking. Grown-ups can be really rude sometimes.

We got to the top and I ran as fast as I could to the shoe department.

'Second Floor-*ah*. Menswear-*ah*, Shoes-*ah*, Gentlemen's Hairdressing-*ah* . . .'

I'd have been better off staying in the lift. Oh no! The clock in the shoe department said twenty-five to. Fifteen minutes late. What was my mum going to say?

'Hello, love, did you have a nice time?'

She wasn't cross.

'Yeah, great . . .'

I couldn't understand it.

'Seventy-one . . . Ticket number seventy-one . . .'

That was why. They hadn't reached us. I was so lucky.

'I've been watching the British Yo-yo Champion. He let me have a go.'

She was reading her *Woman's Weekly*.

'That's nice . . .'

'I was quite good at it.'

'Were you, love . . .?'

She wasn't really listening.

'Yeah. They've got a competition next Saturday to find the yo-yo champion. The winner'll get ten pounds and a cup . . .'

I was just about to tell her that they cost half-a-crown and ask if I could have one when I heard someone calling my name. It was Keith Hopwood. He was with his mum and dad. Keith's dad's ever so small, not much bigger than Keith, and his mum's huge. They looked a bit like Laurel and Hardy. Mrs Hopwood was carrying two big carrier bags and was puffing and blowing. She put her shopping down and sat next to my mum.

'Eeh, I could do without buying shoes this morning, I can tell you. Has your lad been nagging you as well?'

My mum wasn't sure what she was on about.

'How do you mean?'

Mrs Hopwood slipped off her shoes and wiggled her toes about.

'These blessed black suede crêpes they're all wearing.'

'Ticket number seventy-two . . .'

My mum looked at me. Mrs Hopwood was still rubbing her foot.

'Still, if they've all got them what can you do? You can't say no, can you . . .?'

They looked great. I walked up and down like the assistant manager told me.

'They're very durable, madam. Last for ever. We've sold masses of them.'

I didn't ask my mum to buy me a yo-yo. I'd got my black suede crêpes. That was enough.

On the Monday I wore them to school and I felt really good. Arthur Boocock was wearing his. So was Tony, and David Holdsworth and Kenny Spencer and Gordon Barraclough. Keith Hopwood wasn't. They'd sold out. I'd got the last pair. Even Norbert had got some. He'd got them from Crabtree's on the Friday night after school. We looked at him. He knew what we were all thinking.

'I didn't nick 'em, you know. My mam got 'em for me.'

He must have been telling the truth. Even Norbert couldn't pinch a pair of shoes . . . I don't think . . .

'I nicked this though.'

He put his hand in his pocket and pulled out a yo-yo. It was yellow, just like the one Don Martell had been using.

'This feller was demonstrating 'em. All different tricks. There's a competition on Saturday. I can't do it though, I'm useless.'

I could.

'I can. Let's have a go.'

Norbert gave me the yo-yo. I wound up the string and slipped it on my big finger. Everybody was watching. Flick! The yo-yo came out of the back of my hand, went down the string and spun nicely. I lowered it to the floor, nice and slow, and 'walked the dog'. Flick! The yo-yo went up in the air. Flick! It rolled up the string and I caught it. Everybody was really impressed and Norbert said I could keep it.

'I don't want it, I can't even make it go up and down. Anyway, I nicked something better.'

He rummaged about in his pocket again and this time

he brought out a grey crayon. He's so stupid, Norbert, he'd risk getting caught for a crummy crayon.

'It's not a crummy crayon. It's a good trick, this. I'll show you. Someone look out for Bleasdale.'

We had Latin next and Bleasdale was always late. Norbert got on a chair and started drawing on one of the windows. It was a good trick. When he'd finished it looked like the window had been smashed. It was brilliant, dead realistic. Bleasdale didn't notice it, he just told us to open our books at page forty-seven. Everybody started giggling and when he asked us what was the matter we all pointed at the 'broken' window.

'Dear oh dear. Does anybody know how this happened?'

Norbert put his hand up.

'Yes sir, it was me.'

Bleasdale looked surprised.

'Well, Lightowler, your honesty is most commendable but I'm afraid you'll have to go and see the headmaster, tell him what you've done. Off you go, lad.'

We all burst out laughing and Norbert got on the chair, spat on the window and started cleaning it with his mucky handkerchief. Even Mr Bleasdale laughed. He's a good sport.

When my mum got home from work that night I was playing with the yo-yo in the kitchen. I told her that Norbert had given it to me 'cos he didn't want it. Well it was true. I just didn't tell her that he'd pinched it from Crabtree's.

'I'm going to go in for that competition on Saturday.'

'What competition's that, love?'

'At Crabtree's. The yo-yo championship. First prize is a silver cup with your name on and a ten-pound gift token.'

'Oh, that's nice . . .'

I knew my mum hadn't been listening. I went into the front room to practise. I practised every night that week. You've got to practise if you want to be a yo-yo champion. Every day after school, I'd go down to Crabtree's and watch Don. Loop the Loop, Baby in the Cradle, Round the World, all sorts of tricks. Then I'd go home and try them out.

That's what I was doing when I broke the blue vase. I couldn't help it. It wasn't my fault. I was practising.

'It wasn't my fault, Mum, I was looping the loop. I can nearly do it now.'

She looked at me with one of her looks and I thought I'd better shut up quick. I knew why she was so mad. The vase had belonged to my grandma.

'That vase belonged to my grandmother – your *great*-grandmother. It's been in our family for years.'

My *great*-grandmother! I'd always thought it had been my grandma's.

'You always said it were my grandma's.'

'It was and your great-grandma's before her but it doesn't matter now, does it? It's broken.'

She started picking up the pieces.

'Maybe you could glue it together . . .'

She gave me another look.

'I'm sorry, Mum. I didn't mean to break it. It was an accident.'

'Just be careful with that yo-yo. I don't want any more accidents.'

I wouldn't have minded but I wanted to win the yo-yo competition for her, not for me. Well that's not really true. I wanted to be the Yo-yo Champion, 'course I did, but I'd decided that if I won I was going to use the ten-pound

95

voucher to buy her a pearl necklace. She'd been looking at it in the jewellery department after we'd bought my shoes.

On the Friday I was in the kitchen practising Baby in the Cradle – that's when you have to get the string in your left hand and make a triangle shape and then rock the yo-yo to and fro inside the triangle. Don Martell makes it look dead easy but it's not, it's one of the hardest. Anyway, I was in the kitchen practising when the front doorbell rang. It turned out to be Norbert. He walked straight in. He never waits to be asked, doesn't Norbert.

'My mam's not back from work and I've lost my key.'

He usually kept it on a string round his neck.

'It must've come off when I had that fight with Barraclough.'

He's always fighting with Gordon Barraclough, they hate each other. He saw the yo-yo in my hand.

'Hey, do that walking the dog again.'

We went into the kitchen and I did Walking the Dog. Then I did the Loop the Loop and Round the World. And I showed him Baby in the Cradle. It was the best I'd ever done it. Norbert couldn't believe it.

'How come you're so good?'

'I've been practising.'

And I told him I was going in for the competition at Crabtree's.

'Well if you win you ought to give me half the prize money. It's my yo-yo.'

I told him to sod off and I went through all my tricks again. Norbert had a go but he'd been right, he was useless. Then he brought out his grey crayon.

'Hey, do you want to play a good trick on your mam?'

He looked around the kitchen.

'We'll do it on the mirror.'

We've got a mirror on the wall above the fireplace and Norbert stood on a chair.

'I did this on my mam and it didn't half fool her.'

He started drawing and when he'd finished it looked ever so realistic. It really looked like the mirror was broken.

'When does your mam get back from work?'

I put the chair back and looked at the mirror again. It was brilliant.

'About quarter past six.'

'You watch her face when she walks in. You'll have a real good laugh.'

I didn't see her face when she came in and I didn't have a real good laugh.

After I'd practised my yo-yo for a bit and lit the fire and peeled the potatoes for my mum, Norbert and me went out to play tip and run in the back alley. We only played for about ten minutes 'cos Norbert hit the ball into Mrs Chapman's and she wouldn't give it back.

'I'm sick of your balls coming over here. I've told you before. Now go away!'

She used to be nice, Mrs Chapman. She used to give us sweets and biscuits and let us go in her garden to fetch our ball. That was before Mr Chapman died. Now she's narky. Anyway Norbert went off home and I went in.

'Is that you?'

My mum was back. I couldn't wait to see her face. She came into the hall from the kitchen and I saw her face. It was like thunder.

'You and that bloody yo-yo . . .!'

I'd never heard her swear before. I was shocked.

'What's up?'

'What's up? . . . What's up! You've smashed my mirror, that's what's up!'

Oh no, she really thought it was broken. And she thought I'd done it with my yo-yo.

'Mum, it's all right, honest. I'll show you.'

I went past her into the kitchen. I'd wipe off the crayon, show it was a joke and we'd have a real good laugh . . . It wasn't there. The mirror had gone. All that was there was a mark on the wall where it had been hanging.

'Where is it? Where's the mirror?'

My mum was shaking she was so cross.

'Where do you think it is? In the dustbin. A cracked mirror's no good to me.'

In the dustbin! I couldn't believe it. Stupid Norbert and his stupid jokes.

'And don't go looking for that blessed yo-yo – that's on the fire.'

On the fire! My yo-yo! I looked and there it was, melting. My yellow yo-yo. I could just make out the 'LU' of 'LUMAR'. I felt sick. I ran out to the dustbin. Everything would be all right. I'd get the mirror, clean it up, tell my mum how Norbert had done it with his trick crayon and we'd have a real good laugh. And I was sure my mum would take me down to Crabtree's first thing in the morning and get me another yo-yo.

I looked in the dustbin and there it was – in pieces. Smashed to smithereens. My mum must have been in a hell of a temper when she threw it away.

We did go down to Crabtree's next morning, but not to

buy a yo-yo. A letter came for my mum in the post. She read it, said 'Wonderful' and handed it to me. It was from the headmaster.

> *Dear Parents,*
>
> *It has come to my notice that a number of boys have taken to coming to school wearing suede crêpe shoes similar to those favoured by so-called 'Teddy Boys'. I do not consider this to be appropriate footwear for school, nor outside school for that matter, and I am writing to ask you to ensure that your son wears regulation school shoes.*
>
> *Any boy who persists in coming to school wearing suede crêpe shoes will be sent home.*
>
> *I would request your co-operation in this matter.*
>
> *Yours sincerely,*
>
> *J. A. Ogden B.Sc.*
> *Headmaster*

While we were waiting for our turn to buy some 'proper' school shoes I went down to the toy department. Copper-nob won the yo-yo championship. He wasn't half as good as me.

THE BEST DAD

You always knew when Norbert's dad had come out of prison. Norbert would come to school covered in bruises. This time it was on his back. A big red mark that went from his shoulder right across to the bottom of his spine. It looked bad. I saw it when we were getting changed for gym. So did Mr Melrose.

'Turn round, Lightowler.'

Norbert turned round and Melrose frowned.

'Good God, lad. Who did that to you?'

Norbert put on his T-shirt.

'Nobody, sir. I fell off a wall.'

Norbert looked at me. He hadn't fallen off a wall. His dad had done it. He hadn't told me but I knew. His dad was always hitting him but Norbert would never tell.

'You fell off a wall?'

You could tell Melrose didn't believe him.

'Take your top off, lad.'

Norbert took his T-shirt off and Melrose had a closer look.

'It doesn't look like you fell off a wall to me. Looks more like someone's hit you with a belt.'

Norbert looked at me again. He didn't have to worry, I wouldn't say anything.

'Who hit you, lad? You can tell me, there's nothing to be frightened of.'

That's where he was wrong. There was one thing for Norbert to be frightened of – his dad. That's why he never told.

He had done once, years ago, at primary school when we were in Miss Taylor's class. He'd been late that morning but nobody had noticed till Miss Taylor was taking the register.

'Patricia Jackson?'

'Here, miss.'

'Trevor Jenkins?'

'Yes, miss.'

'Olwen Knowles?'

'Present, miss.'

I'd hated Olwen Knowles. She used to sit behind me and she was always whispering and giggling and making me turn round and then I'd always get into trouble.

'Stop turning round. Face the front while I'm taking the register. Jacqueline Lambert?'

'Yes, miss.'

I didn't like her either. Jacqueline Lambert! She used to eat with her mouth open and talk at the same time. It was disgusting. That was one of the good things about being at Grammar School. No girls.

'Dennis Leach?'

'Yes, miss.'

Dennis Leach. He'd left in the middle of the next term. He'd jumped off a bus while it was still moving and banged his head. After that he wasn't the same Dennis. He couldn't read any more and he talked funny and spit always used to dribble out of his mouth. He'd left and gone to a special school near Ilkley. He still lives there and his mum and dad and little brother go and visit him at weekends.

Even now when I'm going out on my bike or going to school my mum always says, 'Be careful. Remember what happened to Dennis Leach.' I once heard her telling my Auntie Doreen that he was a vegetable and when I'd asked her what she meant she just said he'd gone a bit simple. I knew that – that was why he'd gone to the special school – but I couldn't see what that had to do with vegetables.

'Mary Lewthwaite?'

'Yes, miss.'

'Norbert Lightowler? . . . Norbert Lightowler?'

He wasn't there.

'Norbert Lightowler?'

'Not here, miss.'

We all used to sort of sing-song it together.

'Not here, miss.'

Miss Taylor had tutted to herself and carried on.

'David Naismith.'

'Yes, miss.'

Just then the classroom door had opened and he'd walked in. We'd all stared at him. Olwen Knowles had giggled. She used to giggle at anything, did Olwen Knowles, but I don't think she'd meant to be nasty. It was seeing Norbert come in like that. He'd got a black eye and his lip was all swollen. He'd looked awful. The only one who hadn't noticed straight away had been Miss Taylor 'cos she was still doing the register.

'Jennifer Parkinson?'

'Here, miss.'

103

'Why are you laughing, Olwen?'

She'd gone red and pointed at Norbert.

'I'm sorry, miss. It's Norbert . . . Look at his face, miss . . .'

She'd looked.

'Norbert! Whatever's happened?'

Norbert hadn't said anything for a minute. He'd looked like he was going to cry. Then he'd blurted it out.

'My dad hit me, miss!'

Miss Taylor had taken him to the headmaster and his mum and dad had been called to the school.

That was the last time Norbert ever said that his dad had hit him.

His mum hadn't come, just his dad, and when he'd turned up Norbert told the headmaster and Miss Taylor that he'd been lying. He said he'd been playing in the park and that he'd fallen out of a tree and that's how he'd hurt his face and he'd blamed it on his dad 'cos he knew he'd have been in trouble for not going straight to school. It was all a lie. He hadn't fallen out of a tree, his dad *had* hit him. I know 'cos Norbert had told me that afternoon, on our way home from school.

'I wasn't gonna say he'd done it when he was standing there looking at me. So I made it up. Said I'd fallen out of a tree.'

He'd sworn me to secrecy. He tells me everything, does Norbert. He says I'm his best friend. I suppose I am really. He hasn't got any others. I just feel sorry for him. I always have, ever since that day when he'd stood there with this black eye going blue and his lip all swollen telling me what had happened in the headmaster's study.

'What did the headmaster say?'

Norbert had wiped his nose on his sleeve and shrugged.

'He made me apologise to my dad.'

That night his dad had hit him again – but not where it showed . . .

'Come on, Lightowler, there's nothing to be frightened of, lad. Who hit you?'

'Nobody, sir . . . Honest . . . I fell off a wall, sir.'

Melrose looked at him. Norbert looked worried. He knew that Melrose didn't believe him. That's why I said it.

'It's true sir, he fell off a wall. I was with him, sir.'

'When?'

'Yesterday, sir.'

What could I do? I hate lying but if Melrose didn't believe Norbert he might take him off to the headmaster like Miss Taylor had done in our old school. And his mum and dad might be called in. I didn't want him to get into trouble with his dad.

'He just slipped, sir. We was playing "dares", sir . . .'

Now I couldn't tell if Melrose believed *me*.

'*Were* playing dares. You *were* playing dares.'

'Yeah, we was, that's how he hurt his back, sir . . .'

I hate being Norbert's best friend. He's not *my* best friend, Tony's my best friend. But Norbert hasn't got anybody so I have to help him.

'I dared him to walk on Pickersgill's wall, sir.'

Norbert looked at me like I'd gone mad. It was sort of true. We had walked on Pickersgill's wall, but it was a few weeks back and it was me that had fallen, not Norbert. Pickersgill's is a big garage near our school. We go past it on our way home and there's a high wall with a sign saying

105

TRESPASSERS WILL BE PROSECUTED and all along the top there's bits of green glass to stop people climbing on it and we're always climbing on it. Norbert had dared Tony and me to walk on it. Tony hadn't 'cos he'd remembered his mum was taking him to the doctor for his athlete's foot and he'd gone straight home. So Norbert and me dared each other and that's when I'd fallen. I hadn't hurt myself too bad, just grazed my knee and my elbow. But I'd ripped my blazer and my mum had gone mad when I'd got home.

'I don't know what you get up to at school! Look at this!'

She'd spread the blazer out on the kitchen table trying to work out the best way to mend it.

'How did you do it?'

I hadn't said anything. I wasn't going to tell her that I'd done it climbing Pickersgill's wall. Then she'd looked up and pointed her finger at me.

'Have you been fighting?'

'No . . .!'

I'd been so pleased to be able to tell her something that wasn't a lie.

' . . . I haven't been fighting.'

'Are you sure? If you've been fighting, young man, I'd rather know.'

'Mum, I've not been fighting. Honest.'

Well, it was the truth. I hadn't done it fighting. If my mum'd said to me 'Did you do it climbing Pickersgill's wall?' I'd have said yes 'cos I don't like lying.

'How did you do it then?'

I still didn't say anything . . . I sort of shrugged – but I didn't say anything, I didn't lie. But I was lying now to

106

Melrose. I had to, to protect Norbert. He was looking at us. He turned to Norbert.

'Is this true, Lightowler?'

'Yes, sir. He dared me so I did it and I fell off. It looks worse than it is, sir.'

Norbert's good at lying. *I* believed him the way he said it.

'Bit of an idiotic thing to do, don't you think, climbing high walls that have got bits of glass embedded in them?'

We both nodded.

'Yes, sir.'

'Yes, sir.'

'Especially when the Head made an announcement about it in assembly last week . . .'

Had he? I hadn't known that. When?

'Only last Friday the headmaster told the whole school that he'd had complaints from Pickersgill's garage about boys climbing on their wall . . .'

Last Friday? I hadn't heard him make any announcement . . .

'And he made it quite clear what would happen if any boys were caught doing it again . . .'

Last Friday . . .? Last Friday . . .?

'They would be severely punished!'

I remembered now, I hadn't been in assembly last Friday. I'd been late for school 'cos we'd had a leak in the bathroom and my mum had told me to wait at home for Mr Cranley, the plumber.

'I can't take time off work – you'll have to be here to let him in.'

'But Mum, I'll be late for school. I'll get into trouble.'

'Don't worry, it's an emergency.'

And she'd given me a note for Mr Bleasdale explaining about the leak and everything.

'Now once Mr Cranley gets here you can go straight to school. All you have to do is let him in and show him where the leak is.'

I'd been quite pleased. We have maths first thing on a Friday and I didn't mind missing it. But Mr Cranley had turned up not long after my mum had gone so all I'd missed was blooming assembly. I'd got to school just as everybody was filing out and nobody'd blooming noticed. I hadn't even had to give the blooming note in. You can be sure any other time somebody would have noticed and I'd have been in trouble.

'So – you're both in big trouble, aren't you?'

We nodded.

'Yes, sir.'

'Yes, sir.'

He blew his whistle.

'Right, you lot, while I'm gone, three times round the playground . . .'

While he was gone? Where was he going? I was hoping it wasn't what I thought it was.

'I've got to go and see the headmaster for a few minutes.'

It was. He was going to tell the headmaster. It wasn't fair. I'd only been trying to help Norbert. David Holdsworth put his hand up.

'Sir, it's raining.'

'*Four* times round the playground . . .'

Everybody jeered and Kenny Spencer asked Holdsworth why he didn't keep his trap shut.

'Five times for you, Spencer!'

Everybody laughed and Melrose turned to me and Norbert.

'You two, follow me. Lightowler, put your top on.'

The gym is separate from the rest of the school and we followed Melrose across the playground to the main building. He was walking so fast that we had to run to keep up with him.

I couldn't believe it. We were being taken to the headmaster for something we hadn't done. We had climbed on Pickersgill's wall, yes, but that had been ages ago, nothing to do with the headmaster's announcement last Friday. Why hadn't I kept my mouth shut? Just 'cos I felt sorry for Norbert. Well, I felt sorry for myself now and I wasn't going to be his best friend any more.

The others were on their first lap. Arthur Boocock and Gordon Barraclough were leading – as usual. They're the best at sport and they're Melrose's favourites. Boocock's the best at running and Barraclough's the best at football and they're both blooming good at cricket.

'That's it, Arthur, Gordon. Show them how it's done, lads.'

That's it, Arthur, Gordon. Show them how it's done! Blooming Melrose. It was 'cos it was Melrose that I'd stuck up for Norbert. Melrose is always picking on him. Well, he'll have to stick up for himself from now on. And why was his dad always hitting him anyway? If he hadn't got such a horrible dad none of this would have happened. I'd hate to have a dad like Norbert's ... If I *had* a dad. Arthur and Gordon were miles ahead now. Kenny Spencer was next, then Duncan Cawthra, but they were nowhere near. At the back Keith Hopwood was strolling along talking to Douglas Bashforth.

'Hopwood! Bashforth! Get moving! Put some effort into it!'

They both groaned and started running. Slowly. Arthur and Gordon would be lapping them in a couple of minutes. It's no wonder that they're so good at sport – their dads are good at it. Gordon's dad once had a trial for Manchester United and Arthur's does cross-country running. At Sports Day last year they came first and second in the fathers' race. Gordon says his dad's going to win this year 'cos he's been doing special training but Arthur says he hasn't got a chance.

'He might be good at football, your dad, but my dad's best at running. He won last year and he's gonna win this year.'

'No he won't, 'cos my dad's best.'

'I bet you half-a-crown.'

'You're on!'

So they've bet each other half-a-crown. Who cares? It doesn't mean much, the fathers' race, if you haven't got a dad.

We got to the main building and followed Melrose up the corridor to the headmaster's study. He knocked and a couple of seconds later a green light came on saying ENTER.

'You two wait here.'

As soon as he closed the door I turned to Norbert but before I could say anything he called me an idiot.

'Y'what?'

'Why did you have to go and tell him it was Pickersgill's wall I fell off? Idiot!'

110

'*I* didn't know, did I? I wasn't in assembly last Friday. I was only trying to help you. I wish I hadn't now!'

Norbert went quiet. 'I know. It's not your fault.'

'No, it's bloody well not, it's your rotten dad's fault! He shouldn't bloody hit you!'

That's when he thumped me. Well, he didn't thump me really, more sort of pushed me away. But it was what he said . . . I couldn't believe it.

'At least it's better than not having a dad!'

How could he say that? I wanted to say to him, how can you say that? Your dad hits you. He belts you. He's always belted you. And you daren't tell anybody 'cos he'd belt you even more. And you think that's better than not having a dad? How can you say that? But I couldn't speak. I just couldn't get the words out. And I didn't have to. It was as if he could tell what I was thinking.

'He's still my dad, in't he? He's still my dad . . .'

The door opened and Melrose came out.

'When you've seen the Head come straight back to the gym.'

'Yes, sir.'

'Yes, sir.'

Melrose went. Me and Norbert waited there. I didn't say anything. I didn't even look at him. I was mad with myself. I'd got myself into trouble for sticking up for him and here was Norbert sticking up for his dad. I couldn't understand it. It wasn't true. It can't be better than not having a dad. I was better off having no dad than a dad like his. I must be. I'd hate to have a dad like his.

111

The green ENTER light came on and we entered. The headmaster went mad with us.

'What were the two of you thinking of . . .?'

Neither of us said anything.

'Well . . .?'

'Don't know, sir . . .'

'Don't know, sir . . .'

'What did I say in assembly last Friday . . .? Eh . . .? What did I say? Anybody playing in the vicinity of Pickersgill's garage will be severely punished!'

'Yes, sir.'

'Yes, sir.'

I thought about telling him that I hadn't been in assembly last Friday but it wouldn't have made any difference. He'd have just said we shouldn't have been there in the first place . . . and I'd have probably got into more trouble for not giving the note in . . . Anyway Norbert had been in assembly so there was no excuse.

'Have either of you got anything to say before I punish you?'

'No, sir.'

'No, sir.'

He went to the cupboard. Oh no! I knew from other lads what he kept in there. He brought it out. The cane! We were going to get the cane. It wasn't fair. I hadn't done anything wrong and we were getting the cane . . .

I thought about it. For a split second I thought about it – 'Sir, he didn't fall off Pickersgill's wall. We were nowhere near Pickersgill's wall. His dad hit him. His dad's always hitting him . . .' I looked at Norbert. Maybe he'd tell him . . .

Tell him, Norbert, tell him . . .! But he didn't. He just stared straight ahead.

'Right, who's going first?'

I wanted to get it over with. *I* wanted to go first.

'Me, sir.'

But Norbert already had his hand up.

'Right, Lightowler. Bend over, lad.'

Oh no, I'd thought it was going to be on my hand. We'd only got our gym shorts on. It was going to hurt even more. This was the worst day of my life. Norbert bent down and the headmaster lifted the cane up in the air. I couldn't watch. I looked away and closed my eyes. It whooshed through the air and I felt sick as I heard it hit him. What was I going to feel like when it was my turn?

I took a deep breath. My teeth were clenched together like anything. I turned to take Norbert's place but he was still bent down and the cane was up in the air again. Whoosh! This time I saw it. He hit him as hard as he could. He's going to do this to me next, that's all I could think of, he's going to do it to me.

'Last one, Lightowler.'

Another one? Whoosh! Three times! I'm going to be caned three times! I couldn't believe it . . .

'Well done, lad.'

'Well done'? What did he mean, 'well done'? 'Cos he didn't cry? 'Cos he didn't shout out? Is that what he means by 'well done'? If I cry or scream does that mean I won't have done well? Does it mean I'll get an extra one for not 'doing well'? I felt sick.

'OK, lad. Bend over.'

I couldn't believe this was happening to me. It was like I

was in a dream. Whoosh . . .! It was the worst pain I'd ever felt.

Whoosh . . .! I thought I was going to throw up. All I'd tried to do was to stop Norbert getting hit by his dad and here I was getting hit by the headmaster.

Whoosh . . .! The last one. It was over. I think he said 'Well done, lad', I couldn't remember.

We didn't talk on the way back to the gym. But just as we were going in Norbert mumbled something.

'He only hits me when he's been drinking you know . . . my mam says he can't help it . . .'

I could only just make out what he said. I didn't care anyway.

'I don't care, it's nowt to do with me.'

'He's all right most of the time . . .'

'I said I don't care. And it's not true, Lightowler, I'd rather have no dad than one like yours, so you can sod off!'

Once we'd got back Norbert was his same old self, laughing and joking and mucking about. By breaktime it all seemed to be forgotten. Things like that don't bother him. He's used to being in trouble, I suppose. He's used to being hit as well. Me, it was all I could do to stop myself from crying all day. Well I wasn't going to stick up for him any more, I knew that, and he could stop thinking I was his best friend, and I didn't care what he said – I'd rather have no dad than one like his . . . But after a couple of days we were pals again and *I* forgot about it too. Until Sports Day.

Arthur's dad didn't win the fathers' race on Sports Day. Nor did Gordon's dad. Norbert's dad won it. Easily. I watched Norbert run up to him afterwards and give him a big hug.

'You're the best dad in the world, the best dad!'

And, for a moment, I thought maybe Norbert was right. Maybe it is better to have a dad like that than no dad at all . . . But I only thought it for a moment.

THE SWAP

PART ONE

I'd never seen Norbert cry before. Never. I've seen him *nearly* cry lots of times, like in the Easter holidays when we'd gone speedway riding up at Hockley quarry and he'd crashed into me on David Holdsworth's bike and he'd had to have five stitches in his leg. He didn't cry then. *I'd* cried and I was only bruised. And David Holdsworth had cried because the front wheel of his bike had got buckled. But Norbert hadn't cried. Norbert never cries. Not even when Melrose picks on him. Melrose is always making fun of Norbert, making him look a fool in front of everybody, and we all laugh as if it's all in good fun. I laugh as well but I don't like it. It makes my stomach churn because you can see that Melrose isn't doing it in fun. He does it 'cos he doesn't like Norbert. You can see it in his eyes. Well, I can. Like that time at Green Lane swimming baths. That's where we go once a fortnight for lessons. I hate it. It's always freezing cold and the water makes your eyes sting and I'm scared stiff of swimming because I can't swim. Anyway we were all getting into our trunks and Melrose was walking up and down, watching, like he always does, when suddenly his voice boomed out, echoing all round the swimming pool.

'You could grow potatoes in between those toes, lad!'

We all peeped out of our cubicles. I couldn't see who Melrose was talking to but I didn't need to.

'When did you last wash those feet, Lightowler? They're black bright. Come out here, lad, let everybody have a look. Gentlemen, come and look at Mr Lightowler's feet.'

Norbert came out of his cubicle and we all gathered round to look at his dirty feet. I felt ever so sorry for him, everybody staring while he stood there in his old-fashioned underpants. *They* didn't look too clean either. They were more grey than white. Melrose was looking at Norbert with a sort of sarcastic sneer on his face.

'Those underpants look like they could do with a wash as well.'

Melrose laughed and turned to us and we all laughed. I laughed but only because the others laughed. Norbert didn't, he just stared back at him.

'No, sir, clean on this morning. They're just old. They used to be my brother's.'

If it had been me I'd have been in tears by now, but not Norbert. He didn't even cry when Melrose made him have a shower with everybody watching. Norbert never cries. Never.

But he was crying now, sobbing his heart out. He was at the top end of the playground, in the shelter under the woodwork classroom. He didn't know I was watching him. I wouldn't have been if I hadn't left my anorak behind. We'd been using it as a goalpost when we'd played football after school and I'd already got home before I'd remembered that I'd left it behind. Well I didn't remember, my mum did. She'd bought it at the nearly-new shop for two pounds and she wanted my Auntie Doreen to see it.

'Wait till you see it, Doreen. Two pounds and it looks brand new. Go put it on, love.'

That's when I remembered where it was.

'Er . . . I left it at school.'

'Where?'

I didn't dare tell her where it really was, rolled up in a bundle at the top end of the playground . . . if it was still there. It could have been taken by now.

'I'm not sure . . .' My mum gave me one of her looks. 'I think it's in the cloakroom . . . on my peg . . . I think . . .'

I didn't like lying to my mum, that's why I kept saying 'I think'. It sort of makes it less of a lie. I think.

'It's all right, I'll go back and get it.'

My mum told me not to bother.

'If it's on your peg it'll be safe. It's got your name in.'

Oh sure, it'd be safe if it was on my peg. But it wasn't, was it.

'I've got to go back anyway, Mum, 'cos I've left my maths homework at school. I think . . .'

I ran back as fast as I could.

When I got to school it was deserted but I could see my anorak up at the far end of the playground where I'd left it.

Norbert and David Holdsworth had carried on playing after I'd gone. Trust them to leave it there like that. You'd think one of them could have looked after it for me, brought it in next day. Oh no, not them, they just go and leave it there in the middle of the playground. Any Tom, Dick or Harry could have stolen it. That's what my mum's always saying:

'Don't leave your bike out there. Any Tom, Dick or Harry could steal it.'

Or:

'Close the curtains, we don't want every Tom, Dick or Harry peeping in.'

When I was little I used to wonder who this Tom, Dick or Harry was. It used to worry me a bit because the man from the proo was called Tom. Why would he want to peep into our living room? Why would he want to steal my bike? And what was a proo? He used to come every Monday night and say, 'Tell your mam it's Tom from the proo.' And my mum would give him some money and he'd write in a little book. He doesn't come any more. It's Mr McCracken from the Prudential who calls and I know what the money's for now. You get it back when you're old or if you fall under a bus. My mum explained it all to me. I know what Tom, Dick or Harry means too. But it's funny how you don't understand these things when you're young.

I was putting my anorak on and thinking what a good job it was that Norbert and David had left it there even though it was a selfish thing to do when I heard this funny noise. It made me jump. It was coming from the shelter. At first I thought it was a dog or something. It sounded like a puppy whimpering. I went towards where the noise was coming from and saw him sitting on the ground in the shelter, all huddled up, and he was crying. He didn't see me. He had his head in his hands and was sobbing into his knees. He was mumbling something over and over but I couldn't make out what he was saying. I'd never seen Norbert cry and I didn't want him to see me watching him so I went back out into the playground. I leaned against the wall and listened. I didn't know what to do. I wanted to help him, ask him what the matter was, but then he'd know I'd seen him and he'd hate that. I couldn't just go home though, could I? I

120

couldn't just leave him there, crying like that. He'd been all right when we'd been playing football and that was less than an hour ago. What had happened? Maybe he'd had a fight with Holdsworth? No, that wouldn't make Norbert cry. Norbert never cries ... Well, he was crying now. Sobbing his heart out.

I was just about to go back into the shelter and ask him what had happened when I stopped and listened. I could make out what it was he'd been mumbling all this time.

'Bloody Melrose ... Bloody Melrose ... Bloody Melrose!'

What had Melrose done now? What had happened?

'Bloody Melrose ... Bloody exchange – he can stick his rotten blooming exchange!'

I knew why he was crying now and there was nothing I could do. He was crying because he can't go on the school exchange. We're all going, all the boys in our year – except Norbert. Melrose arranged it. We'd all got a letter to take home to our parents. I'd given it to my mum as soon as she'd got back from work.

'What's this? You're not in trouble, are you?'

'No!'

Why does my mum always have to think I'm in trouble? Mind you, the last letter I'd brought home had been from Mr Bleasdale about me messing about in his Latin lesson. It hadn't even been my fault. We'd been playing the game where something gets passed round the class and if you've got it when the bell goes you're the loser. This time the grot was an old woolly hat that Norbert had found in the playground. I hadn't wanted to play but you've got no choice if you get landed with the grot and I got landed with it right at the end of the lesson. I knew the bell was going to go any second. I had to get rid of it. Everybody was sniggering and a few of them, mainly Norbert and Arthur Boocock and Barraclough, were doing the chant.

'Grot! Grot! Grot! Grot . . .!'

I threw the grot just as Bleasdale looked up with his good eye.

'Who's making that noise— Who threw that?'

And then the bell had gone and Keith Hopwood had ended up with the grot. I was sorry it had landed on his desk 'cos he's got a stammer. I'd got extra Latin, a letter to take home and a telling-off from my mum . . .

'It's from Mr Melrose. It's about going on a school exchange.'

She screwed up her eyes and held the letter a bit further away.

'Get my glasses would you, love? They're on the sideboard.'

I could see it was in purple stencil, like our exam papers – sometimes the writing's a bit smudged. I gave my mum her glasses and sat in the wicker chair while she read it through. Then she went 'hmm' and read the letter out loud.

Dear Parents,

The boys in the first year have the opportunity to share an exchange for one week with St Augustine's Grammar School in Greenford, just outside London. At the moment the week suggested would be the first week in May and we are at the stage now where we need to know how many families would be interested.

*Whilst there will be many exciting trips, visits to
Westminster Abbey and the Houses of Parliament,
the Tower of London . . .*

The Tower of London. It sounded great.

'The Tower of London? It sounds great. Can I go,
Mum?'

'Hang on, love, let me finish reading it.'

. . . *Whilst there will be many exciting trips, visits to
Westminster Abbey and the Houses of Parliament, the Tower
of London* – She smiled at me. She was going to let me go,
I could tell. She always smiles like that when she's being nice
– *Madame Tussauds . . .*

'Madam Two Swords! That's a waxworks, Mum, it's
famous!'

My mum told me to calm down and carried on.

. . . *the Tower of London, Madame Tussauds and pos-
sibly a tour round the Lyons Tea Factory (Mr Bleasdale is
waiting to hear from his brother-in-law who works there), it
will be very much a working holiday with set projects and
field work, and each boy will be expected to keep a daily
diary . . .*

She took her glasses off and gave me one of her looks.

'You see. It's not a fancy holiday you'll be going on.
You're going to have to work. You'll be having set projects
and field work and I'll want to see this diary when you get
back. I'll want you to take it seriously.'

I didn't know what field work was but I didn't care. I
just knew I wanted to go on this exchange. I wanted to see
Westminster Abbey and the Tower of London and Madam
Two Swords.

''Course I will.'

'Right. Well think on.'

She put her glasses back on and carried on reading.

. . . *The cost*—

'Mum, if it's a lot of money I'm not that bothered . . .'

'Shut up and listen.'

*. . . I know that this is what will be uppermost in all
your minds, especially in these stringent times. Apart
from the fares to London (train or charabanc, still to
be decided) and modest pocket money, the cost will
be minimal because while our boys are down in
London the boys from St Augustine's will stay with
you, the parents. Your own day-to-day arrangements
will be unaffected since your visitors will keep the
same school hours as your sons and vice versa.*

*This will be an exchange in the true meaning of
the word.*

*If you would like your son to be included in the
St Augustine School exchange would you please let
me know by Friday of this week together with a two
pound deposit. (Non-returnable.)*

Yours faithfully,

Brian T. Melrose Cert. Ed.
(Head of Sport)

That's when it dawned on me.

I thought I'd be going to stay with a lad from this St

Augustine's school and then he'd come back and stay with me and my mum. But we were never going to see each other.

'So I'll never see the lad who stays here? We'll just swap for a week.'

My mum smiled.

'That's right – and with a bit of luck I'll get a nice young man who'll keep his room tidy and make his bed on a morning. That'd be a grand swap.'

I didn't go back and help Norbert, I set off for home. There was nothing I could do. Poor Norbert. But I couldn't understand it. When Melrose had told him that morning that he wouldn't be going on the exchange he hadn't seemed bothered.

'I don't care. I've been to Fountains Abbey. I bet Westminster Abbey in't half as good as that. And who wants to go round a boring tea factory with Bleasdale's boring brother-in-law? Melrose can stick his blooming exchange. I'm not bothered.'

It must have all been an act. He'd brought his non-returnable two pounds in along with everybody else. He'd wanted to go on the exchange. Everybody wanted to go. But then we'd got another letter to take home.

Dear Parents,

<u>School Exchange – Sleeping Arrangements</u>
Please note it will be expected that each boy visiting from St Augustine's will have a bedroom to himself during his week's stay in your home. Likewise our lads will be shown the same courtesy whilst staying with the St Augustine families. This is a condition of the

exchange and is non-negotiable. I am aware that a
number of our boys share with their siblings but I am
sure that suitable arrangements can be made for one
week in order to accommodate our guests.

If any parents have any questions or worries please
do not hesitate to contact me at the school.

I would like to take this opportunity to remind all
parents that the rest of the money must be handed in
by next Monday.

Yours faithfully,

Brian T. Melrose Cert. Ed.
(Head of Sport)

'What are siblings, Mum?'

'Brothers and sisters.'

'Oh.'

Well I was all right. I haven't got any brothers or sisters,
I sleep in my own room. So does David Holdsworth. He's
got an older brother but he's married and lives in Doncaster.
Keith Hopwood shares with his little brother and his mum
and dad are going to move him in with his sister while Keith
is on the exchange. That's what most people are doing, just
moving everybody around for the week. Except Norbert.
He's got so many brothers and sisters that he doesn't just
share a bedroom, he shares a bed. Norbert had told Melrose
that his mum could arrange for the guest to have his own
bed but he'd have to share the room with two of his brothers.

'And my mum says my little sister can go in with her
for the week.'

Melrose had just sucked in his breath and shaken his head.

'I'm sorry, Lightowler, it's not on. I'll have to take your name off the list. I'm sorry, lad.'

I don't think he was sorry. Melrose doesn't like Norbert. I reckon he's glad Norbert's not going.

'Sir?'

'Yes, Lightowler?'

'My mum says can she have her two pound back?'

Melrose had said it was supposed to be non-returnable but muttered something about 'in the circumstances' and he got it back. And Norbert hadn't seemed bothered at all.

But he *was* bothered because there he was, sitting in the playground, crying his eyes out. Poor Norbert.

When I got home my mum made me stand in the middle of the living room while she and my Auntie Doreen admired my nearly new anorak.

'Now look at that, Doreen, two pounds. It looks brand new. It'll be ideal for this school trip.'

If my mum had known that half an hour before it had been lying in the playground being used as a goalpost, she wouldn't have been too pleased. I was still thinking about Norbert.

'Norbert's not going on the exchange now.'

She saw something on the sleeve and brushed it off with her hand.

'Oh, what's that, love?'

I took my anorak off and hung it in the hall. I didn't want my mum to look too closely in case there were any more dirty marks.

'Well, you know that letter we got from Melrose—'

'*Mr* Melrose!'

'Yeah, all right. Well, you know he said that everybody has to have their own bedroom? Well Norbert shares with two of his brothers. That's why he can't go.'

My mum looked at my Auntie Doreen.

'I'm sorry, I don't want to be uncharitable but I think it's a blessing in disguise. I wouldn't like to think of a son of mine spending a week in a house like that. And I wouldn't want someone like Norbert Lightowler spending a week in my house either. I'm sorry, I know it's not his fault, I feel sorry for the lad having a family like that, but ... well, I think it's for the best. Do you fancy another cup, Doreen?'

They went into the kitchen and I could hear my mum telling my Auntie Doreen all about the Lightowlers. How mucky their house is, how the kids are always in trouble with the police, how *he's* in and out of prison. I suppose she meant Norbert's dad. My mum was right though. I mean it's not Norbert's fault but his house is horrible. You couldn't expect anybody coming on the exchange to stay there. I wouldn't ...

Dear Peter,

Thanks for your letter which I got yesterday. It was very nice to get your letter. I am looking forward to coming to stay at your house and meeting all your family. They all sound very nice. I hope you will enjoy staying at my house ...

We'd all got letters from the St Augustine boys and during one English lesson we had to write back. Melrose told us we had to write at least a page. He made Norbert write a letter even though he wasn't going just to give him something to do in the lesson. The lad I'm swapping with is called Peter Jarvis. He's got an older brother called Stephen and an older sister called Rosemary who's at teacher training college. His father works in insurance and his mother works for charity sometimes but doesn't get paid for it. He's in the school chess team and his favourite subject is chemistry. I think they must have done their letters at home not in class 'cos he didn't say much else. Just that he was looking forward to the trip and it was a shame we would never meet and that I could use his bicycle.

> ... *I live with my mum and she is looking forward to meeting you. She has made me tidy my bedroom up so that it will be nice for you. I have got a wireless in my bedroom so you can listen in bed. It used to belong to my grandad but he died two years ago. The Home Service is a bit crackly but not bad. I love listening to the wireless in bed. My favourite is Have a Go with Wilfred Pickles and Up the Pole with Jimmy Jule and Ben Worris. I think they are very funny. I like listening to plays as well but usually I fall asleep before the end or my mum comes in and tells me to switch off and go to sleep. The other night I listened to a play called Night Must Fall and it was a murder play and I was scared stiff and I could not sleep. I had told my mum I had turned it off but I was so frightened I had to own up so I could go into her bed until I fell asleep. I am in 1 Beta and our form master is Mr Bleasdale. He teaches Latin and he has a glass*

*eye. My best friend is Tony Wainwright but he is in 1
Alpha. He is going on the exchange too. All the boys in
our year are going except one. My mum is going to
take you to Ilkley Moor to see the cow and calf. The
cow and calf are two rocks and one is bigger than the
other. The cow is the big one and the calf is the little
one. It is a very famous place and it is great for
climbing there. My mum is going to take you on some
other trips but I won't say where so it will be a
surprise . . .*

Melrose told us to finish 'cos the bell was about to go so I
just wrote that I hated chemistry and I was sorry that we
wouldn't meet and that he could use my bike as well. Then
Melrose collected all the letters to post to St Augustine's.
Except Norbert's. He threw his in the waste-paper basket.

Dear Parents,

<u>School Exchange – Travel Arrangements</u>
*Well, the big day approaches. Could you ensure that
your son is at the school on Saturday at 8.30 a.m. for
an 8.45 departure (prompt).*

*We will be going to Leeds by charabanc and there
we will pick up the 10.25 train to London (King's
Cross). The party will be led by myself, Mr Bleasdale
and Mrs Jolliffe. The St Augustine boys will be arriving
at our school at 5.15 p.m. (approx.) for you to pick
them up.*

*Attached to this letter is a list of clothes required,
etc. As your son will be representing the school, would*

130

you please ensure that his blazer is in a presentable state (buttons, torn pockets, etc). Also on the list is the telephone number at St Augustine's. <u>Please telephone only in a case of emergency</u>. Thank you for your co-operation. Finally, would those who have not paid their outstanding balance please do so by this coming Wednesday as I shall be out of pocket.

Yours sincerely,

Brian T. Melrose Cert. Ed.
(Head of Sport)

'Spencer . . .'

   'Sir.'

'Thompson . . .'

   'Yes, sir!'

'Tordoff . . .'

   'Sir!'

We were all on the coach waiting to go while Mr Bleasdale ticked off our names. Well, not all. Keith Hopwood hadn't turned up, but he's always late for everything. I was sitting next to Tony. Me and my mum had got there early so the two of us could sit together and we were going to sit next to each other on the train as well.

   'Wainwright . . .'

I nudged him and Tony put his hand up.

   'Present, sir!'

Everybody laughed and Mr Bleasdale smiled. He's quite nice really.

   'Walsh . . .'

Everybody was so excited and talking to each other.

'Walsh . . .'

Brian Walsh was chatting away to Kenny Spencer and Duncan Cawthra. I leaned over and nudged him.

'Hey Walshie, he's called your name.'

I suppose it's hard for Mr Bleasdale to see properly when he's only got one eye.

'Is Brian Walsh here?'

Walshie stuck his hand up.

'Yes, sir!'

Mr Bleasdale ticked his name off.

'I know you're excited, lads, but keep the noise down and listen for your names. I'm not telling you again . . .'

He'd told us to pipe down about three times already. It was a good job it wasn't Melrose taking our names – he's not as nice as Mr Bleasdale.

All the parents were standing on the pavement waiting to wave us off. I could see my mum talking to Tony's mum and dad. Norbert had turned up as well. He was chewing bubble gum and he had his dog with him, a scrawny, scruffy-looking thing called Nell. He grinned at me and Tony and gave us a thumbs-up. I felt sorry for him.

'I feel sorry for Norbert.'

Tony looked at me.

'Why? He's not bothered. You know Norbert – he doesn't give a damn, does he?'

I knew different. I'd seen him in the playground. I didn't say anything. There was no point. And my mum was right, it was a blessing in disguise. You couldn't expect a stranger to stay at his house.

Suddenly a few of the lads started shouting.

'He's here, sir. Hopwood's here! Come on, Hopwood.' I could see him running towards the coach with his mum and dad and everybody cheered as they bundled him on. Mrs Hopwood was in a right state.

'I'm sorry, Mr Melrose, you know what the buses are like on a Saturday. We had to wait over half an hour . . .'

And the next thing we were on our way. Melrose and Mrs Jolliffe got on and the driver started revving up and everybody on the pavement started waving.

I looked out of the window and my mum gave me a little wave. I gave her a little wave back and she smiled. I smiled as well but I didn't feel like smiling. All of a sudden I felt frightened. I didn't want to go. All these weeks of looking forward to it and now I didn't want to go. I'd never been away from home for this long. She came over and said 'Are you all right?' through the window. Well, she didn't say it, she just moved her lips, but I could tell that's what she was asking. I nodded. But I wasn't all right. It was all I could do to stop myself from crying. It was going to be a week before I was going to see my mum again. I didn't think I could last that long. A whole week without seeing my mum. Norbert was waving as well and I started wishing I was Norbert, staying at home. Lucky Norbert, not having to go away for a week, not having to stay with a family he didn't know. I didn't want to go, I wanted to get off, go home with my mum, but the coach started moving off and everybody began cheering and I could feel the tears behind my eyes. Don't let me start crying, please don't let me start crying.

My mum started running alongside the coach. Why was she doing that? She looked funny. None of the other mums and dads were running alongside. Stop it, Mum, stop it.

133

I looked away. Please stop, Mum, you look silly, you're embarrassing me. I looked back and she was still there, running and waving and wiping her eyes with a hanky. Then thank goodness we started going faster and she slowed down. The coach stopped at some lights and I looked back. All the other mums and dads were walking off but she was still standing there, out of breath, waving and crying.

'Have a nice time, love!'

David Holdsworth and a few of the others went 'Have a nice time, love' and giggled.

'See you in a week, love!'

Why didn't my mum just go? Why didn't the lights change? Change lights, change!! They did change. But not in time. If they'd changed just a few seconds sooner nobody would have heard her.

'Keep an eye on him, Mr Bleasdale. He's all I've got . . .!'

Everybody started laughing, and what made it worse was they were all trying to hold it in. Couldn't she have shouted, 'Keep an eye on him, Mr Melrose' or 'Mrs Jolliffe'? No, she had to shout, 'Keep an eye on him, Mr Bleasdale.' Mr Bleasdale! The only teacher with one eye!

I turned away so nobody could see me crying. I wanted to blow my nose but I couldn't. My mum had packed my hankies in my suitcase.

THE SWAP

PART TWO

I could feel the tears in my eyes. I turned my head away and
looked out of the window so that nobody could see. I think
maybe Tony knew but he didn't say anything, he was talking
to Kenny Spencer across the aisle.

I just kept looking out of the window and everything I
saw made me feel worse. We went past Mrs Allsop's High
Class Hairdressing Salon where my mum goes with my
Auntie Doreen every Saturday afternoon. She'd be going
there that afternoon and it made me feel more sad. We went
past the end of our road and I could feel the tears running
down my face. I wiped them away with my sleeve. If only I
could blow my nose.

I was lucky. Nobody really noticed that I was crying.
They would have done if it hadn't been for Keith Hopwood,
but I was lucky. He threw up. It went everywhere, mostly
over David Holdsworth's blazer. Everybody jumped back
and started shouting.

'Sir, sir! Hopwood's been sick.'

'All over my blazer, sir. It's just been dry-cleaned, my
mum'll go mad!'

Melrose told everybody to calm down and go back to
their places. Holdsworth and Duncan Cawthra said they
couldn't 'cos there was sick on their seats.

'Just sit down – *anywhere*! Use your common sense!'

Melrose was all red in the face and the vein under his eye was throbbing. When that vein throbs you know Melrose is really mad. Hopwood just kept saying he was sorry. He kept saying it over and over. And 'cos of his stutter he could hardly get his words out.

'I'm s-s-sorry, s-sir. I'm e-e-ever so s-s-sorry. Sorry, D-D-David . . .'

And he threw up again, mostly in the aisle, and everyone got out of the way again.

'S-s-sorry, s-sir, I c-couldn't help it . . .'

Mrs Jolliffe had a box of tissues and gave him some and Holdsworth took a few to wipe his blazer. Mr Bleasdale put his *Yorkshire Post* over Hopwood's sick while Mrs Jolliffe put her arm round him.

'Don't worry, Keith, it's not your fault. It's running for the coach, that's what's made you sick. Here, blow your nose.'

Then he started crying.

'No it's n-not. I've been f-feeling sick all n-night 'cos I was nervous about g-g-going. That's w-why I was late, 'cos I d-didn't want to g-go. I d-don't want to g-go now. I w-want to g-g-go home. I want to g-g-go *home* . . .!'

I leaned across and asked Mrs Jolliffe if I could have one of her tissues.

'Help yourself, dear.'

She didn't look round, she was busy looking after Keith. She probably thought I needed to wipe the seat or something so I took a few and blew my nose.

I felt better. Much better. Not 'cos I'd been able to blow my nose but 'cos I knew now that I wasn't the only one who was frightened about going away from home. I bet lots of us were scared but some are just better at hiding it than others.

'I want to g-go h-home, Mrs Jolliffe. P-please let me g-go home. I d-don't w-w-want to go London!'

And he started crying again.

Everybody was looking at him. If Keith hadn't been sick it would have been me everybody would have been looking at and me Mrs Jolliffe would have been comforting.

'Come on, dear, you come and sit with me and we'll have a little talk.'

As she went past I heard her whispering to Bleasdale and Melrose that he'd be all right and to leave it to her. The vein under Melrose's eye was throbbing like anything.

I looked out of the window again. I knew just how Keith was feeling. I'd never felt so sad in all my life. I didn't want to go to on this school exchange either. A whole week before I'd see my mum. And my Auntie Doreen. A whole week staying with strangers. I could feel the tears coming again. No! I wasn't going to cry. I wasn't. I wouldn't let myself. I didn't want everybody looking at me the way they'd all looked at Keith Hopwood. The way *I'd* looked at Keith Hopwood. Then I realised that Tony was looking at me. Looking at me the way *he'd* looked at Keith Hopwood.

'Are you cryin'?'

'No, 'course not.'

He didn't believe me, I could tell.

'Your eyes are all red.'

'I know . . .'

When my Auntie Doreen had come back from the doctor's last Thursday she'd told my mum she'd got an eye infection, con-something, and her eyes were all red.

'. . . I've got an eye infection. I got it off my Auntie Doreen.'

'You look like you've been cryin'.'

'I know. So did my Auntie Doreen.'

I turned away from him and looked out of the window again. We were just going past the GPO. The coach turned onto the Leeds road and headed out of town.

I kept thinking to myself, this time next week it'll all be over. That's how I stopped myself from crying. Whenever something horrible is going to happen to me, like having to have an injection, or having to go to the dentist, that's what I always think. In an hour, in a day, this time tomorrow, it'll all be over, forgotten. Well, it was the same with this blooming rotten school exchange. I just kept thinking to myself, this time next week it'll all be over – we'll be on our way home.

Hopwood was still crying when we'd got to Leeds station, but not as much. More sort of sniffing and he was sucking a barley sugar Mrs Jolliffe had given him. To calm his tummy down. Melrose got up and stood at the front next to the driver.

'We are now at Leeds station.'

We could see we were at Leeds station, there was a big sign that said so. Tony leaned over to me.

'Does he think we can't read?'

I giggled.

'What are you laughing at, lad?'

I could feel myself going red.

'Nothing, sir.'

''Cos if there's something that amuses you, lad, let's share it. Let's all have a bit of a laugh.'

I stared straight ahead at Melrose. Well, not at him, I sort of looked through him, behind him. It was the only way I could stop myself from crying. What was the matter with me? I could feel my bottom lip trembling. The driver winked at me and smiled. I suppose he was trying to cheer me up. I gave him a little smile back.

'Take that grin off your face, lad.'

I did. So did the driver. I don't know whose smile disappeared the fastest, his or mine. He turned round in his seat and started fiddling about with a cloth, wiping all the dials, and I looked down at my feet.

'I'm going to say something now and I shall only say it once. When I or Mr Bleasdale or Mrs Jolliffe is speaking, there will be absolute and total silence while you listen to our instructions. Is that understood?'

Nobody said anything.

'*Is that understood?*'

Everybody jumped, even the driver. He stood up and started polishing his windscreen.

'Yes, sir.'

'Good . . .'

The vein underneath Melrose's eye was throbbing again.

'. . . because only if you listen carefully and follow instructions will we avoid any mishaps and misunderstandings. Is that clear, gentlemen?'

'Yes, sir.'

'Excellent. Now when you get off the charabanc I want you all to line up in twos and I don't want to hear *any talking*. Hutchinson – lead off.'

We all followed each other off and started getting into

139

twos like Melrose had said. But a few of them started arguing. Illingworth wanted to be with Emmott, Emmott wanted to be with Duncan Cawthra, Cawthra was already with David Holdsworth and John Tordoff wanted to be with Tony 'cos they're in the same class and I was telling him that Tony was already with me and Tordoff said when they walked to swimming in twos they were always together and that they sat next to each other in class and I said that had nothing to do with it 'cos Tony was my best friend and we'd been best friends since Primary School . . .

'I said *no talking*! Into pairs – *now!!*'

We all turned and looked for our partners as fast as we could but I couldn't find Tony for a minute and the next thing I knew we were all in twos but Tony was with Tordoff and I'd ended up with Arthur Boocock. I can't stand Arthur Boocock. He's a bully and he's got bad breath. What makes it worse, he comes up right close when he talks to you. His face is always about an inch away. Melrose was standing on the steps of the coach.

'Better . . .'

And he steals, does Boocock. I'm positive he took my Ovaltiney pencil case. I should have put my name in it.

'Now that's what I want to see when I tell you all to line up in twos . . .'

It had disappeared one Friday afternoon and on the following Monday Arthur Boocock turns up with an Ovaltiney pencil case.

'Hey, look what I've got, an Ovaltiney pencil case an' all. It came on Saturday morning. I've scratched my initials inside so it doesn't get mixed up with yours. Look.'

It was mine. It had a dent where I'd dropped it on

140

my Auntie Doreen's kitchen floor. He'd scratched A.B. in my pencil case. But I couldn't prove it. If only I'd put my initials inside.

'I want you to take note of the person you are standing next to because this will be your partner for the week . . .'

Oh no! I didn't want to be with smelly Arthur Boocock every time we lined up . . . This was going to be the worst week of my life.

'Now you will all go with Mr Bleasdale to platform 4. I will follow with the luggage. Do *not* get on the train until you are told to. Mrs Jolliffe – will you take up the rear?'

Mrs Jolliffe was still holding Keith Hopwood's hand. I wondered if they'd be partners for the whole week. I reckoned they'd have to be 'cos there was no one else Hopwood could go with. I'd have rather been with Hopwood than Arthur Boocock. I'd have rather been with Mrs Jolliffe than Arthur Boocock. Spencer put his hand up.

'Sir?'

'Yes, Spencer.'

'What about us suitcases, sir?'

Everybody groaned and jeered and Arthur Boocock shouted, 'Wash your ears out.' He can talk – his ears are black bright. Spencer went all red.

'Do listen, lad. I just said I will bring all the luggage.'

Bleasdale stuck his hand up in the air, shouted 'Follow me' and we all followed. He kept his arm up all the way, shouting 'Left', 'Right', 'Straight on' and we started giggling. We went into the station just as a train was pulling out and the engine driver let out a great blast of steam making us all jump. We started laughing and talking and Mrs Jolliffe told us to be quiet and to keep our eyes on Mr Bleasdale. You

141

could hardly miss him with his hand stuck up in the air like that. He looked stupid. We got to platform 4 and he turned and held up his hand for us to stop. A whole carriage was reserved for our school. We could see Melrose and a porter coming down the platform pulling a trolley with all our cases on.

I felt a bit better. I like trains. I like the smell of the coal burning and the noise and the steam. I didn't like Arthur Boocock though.

'Hey Arthur, will you do us a favour? Will you swap with Tordoff so's I can be with Tony?'

Well, it was worth asking.

'What's wrong wi' me then?'

I don't like you 'cos you've got mucky ears and smelly breath and you're a bully and you stole my Ovaltiney pencil case. That's what I felt like saying.

'Nowt. Tony's my best friend, that's all.'

He smiled at me. Well, it was more of a sneer really.

'What'll you give us?'

He looked down at my blazer. He was staring at my Ovaltiney badge . . . I thought about it but not for very long.

'I'll give you my Ovaltiney badge.'

'All right.'

He held his hand out and I gave it to him. He pinned it on his blazer. It was worth it. I could always send away for another one when I got home. All you need is four Ovaltine labels. When I got home . . . Oh I didn't half wish I was home. He called over to Tordoff.

'Hey, Wing-nut!'

That's his nickname. Wing-nut. Melrose had started it

142

'cos of his sticky-out ears. Now we all call him Wing-nut.
He looked round.

'What?'

'Over 'ere – quick.'

Tordoff frowned.

'Quick!'

He came over, making sure Bleasdale and Mrs Jolliffe
didn't see.

'What do you want?'

Arthur was still pinning the badge onto his blazer.

'You're wi' me.'

Wing-nut didn't know what he was on about.

'Y'what?'

'You're wi' me, you're my partner.'

'I'm not.'

He started to walk back but Boocock got hold of his
arm and showed him his fist.

'Do you want thumping?'

You don't argue with Arthur Boocock. Wing-nut looked
at me and I shrugged as if I had nothing to do with it. Well,
as far as Wing-nut knew, I didn't. I turned to Boocock, all
innocent.

'Er . . . shall I go over there then, Arthur?'

He was still fiddling with my Ovaltiney badge.

'Yeah, push off.'

I shrugged again as if I didn't have a clue what was
going on and went over to Tony. I felt sorry for Wing-nut –
but not that sorry.

When we got on the train there were six of us to a
compartment. In ours we had me and Tony, Holdsworth and
Cawthra and Mrs Jolliffe and Keith who was a bit more

cheerful. She's all right, Mrs Jolliffe. She gave us all a barley sugar to settle our tummies and joined in when we played I-Spy. And after we'd had our sandwiches she gave us an apple each, to clean our teeth.

And when Keith started crying again she told him if he didn't stop she'd put him in the luggage rack. Not nasty. She said it in a kind voice and made him laugh.

'I'm sorry, miss, but I keep thinking about my mum and dad and it makes me cry. I can't help it. I even keep thinking about my little sister and I can't stand her.'

Everybody laughed but I wanted to say, I know what you mean, that's how I feel. And it must've been worse for Keith having a dad and a sister to miss as well. I've only got my mum. And my Auntie Doreen.

'Of course it's a bit frightening when you go away from home for the first time. Everybody's a bit nervous, Keith, but some don't show it as much as others.'

He nodded and took a bite of his apple. I put my hand up and Mrs Jolliffe laughed.

'You're not in class now. You don't have to put your hand up.'

I felt myself go red.

'I just wanted to say that I feel a bit like Keith does. I keep thinking about my mum all the time.'

Mrs Jolliffe smiled.

'You see, Keith. And I wouldn't mind betting that David and Duncan and Tony are feeling a little homesick. Aren't you, boys?'

I don't think they were at all homesick but Mrs Jolliffe gave them a little wink. She made sure Keith couldn't see. They looked at each other.

144

'Yeah . . .'

'A little bit . . .'

And Tony nodded.

'And do you think the boys from St Augustine's aren't feeling nervous? Of course they are. It's only natural. Now who'd like another barley sugar?'

We all put our hands up except Keith. He went to the lavatory. After he shut the sliding door Holdsworth told Mrs Jolliffe that he wasn't really feeling homesick and Cawthra said he wasn't either. So did Tony . . . So did I:

'No, me neither. I just felt sorry for Keith.'

Mrs Jolliffe leaned over and took hold of my hand.

'I know. It was very nice of you. Thank you.'

She squeezed my hand and smiled. I just about managed to smile back. I was such a liar. The others started playing I-Spy again. I didn't feel like it so I got my library book out. But I couldn't concentrate. All I could hear were the wheels on the track, talking to me:

I want to go home . . . I want to go home . . . I want to go home . . . I want to go home . . .

The coach was parked outside St Augustine's.

We were going home. The week was over. All the St Augustine parents were waiting to wave us off. I looked out of the window and I could see Mr and Mrs Jarvis and Stephen, the family I'd swapped with. Mrs Jarvis gave me a little smile and waved and Mr Jarvis took another photo. I smiled. I didn't feel like smiling though. I felt terrible. And so ashamed. I didn't want to go home. It had been the best week of my life . . .

Dear Mum,

It is terrific here. I am having a great time. Mr and Mrs Jarvis are really nice. They have got a Rover 90 car and have taken me to all sorts of places. They have taken me on a picnic in the country and they have taken me to posh restronts twice. They live in a posh house, it is like a mansion and they have got two bathrooms, one for me and Stephen, Peter's brother, and another bathroom inside their bedroom for themselves. There are three toilets in their house. I have got bunk beds and I am sleeping in the top one. Tell Peter. Peter's room is smashing. He has got his own basin in his room and a lovely soft carpet everywhere and his own desk built right across one wall. They have got a lovely garden, it is massive and behind the garden are fields and every night me and Stephen play French cricket and when Mr Jarvis comes home from work he joins in and so does Mrs Jarvis. She is very nice and very pretty . . .

I stopped writing and read the letter. Then I tore it up and started again.

Dear Mum,

We are having a great time. We went to the Tower of London. It was great.

And Westminster Abbey and the Houses of Parliment. They were great. Yesterday we went to

146

*Madam Two Swords except that it is not Two Swords
it is Tussords and it was great . . .*

It wasn't as long as the letter I'd torn up but it was longer
than the one Peter had sent to his mum and dad. Mr Jarvis
had read it out at breakfast.

Dear Mummy, Daddy and Stephen,

*I am having a good time. We went round a wool
factory. It was noisy. Looking forward to seeing you
soon.*

Love,

Peter

I wrote all about Keith Hopwood being homesick and about
Kenny Spencer and Douglas Goodall getting lost in the
underground station and how Melrose went mad and that I
hoped Peter was having a good time. And I put in another
letter for my Auntie Doreen. I didn't say anything about the
lovely house and the massive garden and Peter's smashing
bedroom and going to posh restaurants. I was worried it
might upset her.

The coach started moving off. We were going. Everybody was shouting and waving and Melrose was saying 'All
right, all right, calm down.'

I looked back and I could see Mr and Mrs Jarvis waving.
Stephen was running alongside trying to take a photo. I tried
my best to smile but I could feel the tears coming. I was

going home and I felt miserable. Why did I feel so miserable?
Holdsworth and Cawthra started singing 'One green bottle'
and a few others joined in. Keith Hopwood was one of them.
It was the first time he'd looked happy all week.

We got off the bus at the end of our road and the conductor
handed my mum my suitcase.

'I'll carry that, Mum.'

'You're all right, love.'

We walked towards our house. It felt strange being back.
Everything looked different. So . . . dreary.

'Eeh, it'll be good to have you home. He was a nice
enough lad, that Peter, but he was so quiet. He had nothing
to say for himself, it was like being on my own.'

I walked along next to my mum. We got to our gate.
Peter would be going home in the Rover 90 . . . to his lovely
house . . . I thought about his bedroom and the bunk beds
and the garden.

My mum opened the front door and we went in.

The hall looked so dark. I'd never noticed that before.
And there was a funny smell that I'd never noticed before. A
bit like cabbage. Old cabbage. And it felt so cold.

'Are you glad to be home?'

'Yeah, 'course I am.'

I felt like a real traitor. I wasn't glad to be home. I was
glad to see my mum. 'Course I was. But I wasn't glad to be
home. I kept thinking about Mr and Mrs Jarvis . . . I felt like
a real traitor.

'Let's have a cup of tea and you can tell me all about
your holiday.'

I put the kettle on while my mum unpacked my suitcase.

'What on earth have you got in here . . .'

She was going through all the pockets.

'Old sweet wrappers, empty crisp packets . . . Do you want these comics?'

I told her I'd read them so she bundled them all into a carrier bag and asked me to throw it away.

I went outside to put it in the dustbin. I stood in the backyard and looked around. It all looked so scruffy. Peter would probably be playing French cricket with his dad and Stephen in the garden now . . . I wished *I* was still there. I wished I had a dad and big brother and a big garden and a Rover 90 – and I wished I could stop wishing these thoughts – and a big posh house and a mum like Mrs Jarvis. No! No! I love my mum. Why was I thinking horrible things like this? Why was I feeling homesick for the wrong home? I went to the midden and threw the carrier bag into the dustbin. That's when I saw it. An envelope torn in half with the name 'Jarvis' written on it.

At first I thought it was from Mr and Mrs Jarvis to Peter but then I saw half the address and I realised it was the other way round. It was from Peter to his mum and dad. It was half of a letter. I scrabbled around in the dustbin and after a minute or two I found the other half. I put the two bits of paper together . . .

Dear Mummy and Daddy,

I hate it here. I want to came home. I am missing you all the time. This house is horrible. It is dark and dirty and cold and it smells. Please come and fetch me, I don't want to stay here . . .

149

And he wrote horrible things about my mum, that she was old and ugly, like an old witch and that he couldn't understand what she was saying and the toilet was outside . . .

> *And there's no garden and she's got a sister and they drink tea all the time and she makes me call her Auntie Doreen and I can't understand her either. Please PLEASE let me come home. There are no carpets here. Daddy can come in the car. Please.*
>
> *Love,*
>
> *Peter*
> *XXX*
>
> *Don't be upset when you get this letter.*

I screwed up his letter, threw it in the bin, wiped the tears away with my sleeve and went back in the house. My mum was pouring the water into the teapot.

'Come on, love, your Auntie Doreen'll be here in a minute. We'll all have a nice cup of tea.'

I got the cups and saucers out and put them on the table. My mum smiled at me.

'Are you pleased to be home?'

I put my arms round her and hugged her as hard as I could.

'Yes, Mum – it's lovely . . .'